JOHN BARNES

THE
END

TABLE OF CONTENTS

Chapter 1.   SIGNS OF THE TIMES   1

Chapter 2.   THE CONDITION OF THE WORLD   11

Chapter 3.   KATIE MARTIN   16

Chapter 4.   EXPECTING THE UNEXPECTED   28

Chapter 5.   QUESTIONS   42

Chapter 6.   GETTING CLOSER   50

Chapter 7.   THE CRAZY WORLD WE LIVE IN   59

Chapter 8.   SIGNS   69

Chapter 9.   HOMECOMING   79

Chapter 10. KATIE IS HOT!   97

Chapter 11. AGONY   109

Chapter 12. OUR NEW RELATIONSHIP   115

Chapter 13. CHOICES   127

Chapter 14. MAKING MY CHOICE   140

Chapter 15. MY KATIE CONNECTION   154

Chapter 16. BODY AND SPIRIT   159

Chapter 17. KATIE'S SHOCK   178

Chapter 18. KATIE'S HELL/MY HEAVEN   190

Chapter 19. MY FIRST ASSIGNMENT   197

Chapter 20. CANDELIGHT VIGIL   207

Chapter 21. THE PROTEST   214

Chapter 22. THE FUNERAL   217

Chapter 23. GETTING TO WORK   235

Chapter 24. DISASTERS ON EARTH   248

Chapter 25. PREPARATION TIME   257

Chapter 26. DESTRUCTIVE FORCES   264

Chapter 27. THE DESCENSION   272

CHAPTER 1

SIGNS OF THE TIMES

"Hurry up man—Tyson just texted that all of the stalls in the bathroom are full now," Chandler said. "We need to fill up the bucket before guys get out of there."

While the water filled the five-gallon bucket, I took a dropper of yellow food coloring I had kept in my pocket all morning and dumped the whole thing into the bucket to turn the water yellow.

"Looks like you got that from the toilet," Ben said with a laugh.

He quickly unwrapped a couple chocolate bars to dump into our bucket, and Chandler added a few pieces of toilet paper to put the finishing touches on it.

We had played this joke on freshmen and sophomores in the bathroom four or five times already in the new school year, and we still laughed every time we did it. We were surprised no one had caught us yet.

Chandler carefully took the full bucket out of the janitor's sink and walked down the hall with it to the boy's bathroom, where Tyson was waiting in the last stall.

At West View High School, there are four stalls in each boy's bathroom. As a senior prank on underclassmen, one of us goes into the end stall and waits for the others to bring him the bucket of fake human waste.

I texted Tyson and said we were coming in so he could unlock the door to his stall.

Chandler was careful not to splash any, as he handed the bucket off to Tyson.

Tyson sat the bucket down on the floor quietly, flushed his toilet, waited a few seconds, and yelled, "Oh no, it's overflowing!"

Then he slowly poured the bucket under the stalls so the guys would think they were coming in contact with water from an overflowing toilet.

"Lift your feet!" Tyson yelled, as the yellow water, toilet paper and chocolate bars flowed along the floor by each toilet.

"Gross!" yelled voices in the stalls.

Luckily, there was a drain in the middle, so it would all go down the drain. But whoever was sitting in that second stall would have to watch it all go down by his feet.

"Dude! That was hilarious!" Tyson said, as we ran out the bathroom door.

"Nice teamwork!" Chandler said. "Now get to class," he said as he hurried ahead of us.

"I'll take the bucket back to the janitor's closet," Ben said. "We're going to need it the next time we do this."

That was our idea of a clean joke. The school thinks they have a plumbing problem, so they keep sending plumbers to fix it. But those plumbers have never found anything wrong.

The late bell rang before I got to my world events class. Mr. Lopez liked me, so I didn't have to worry about being a minute late. He was also the assistant football coach and since I was one of the team captains, I hoped I'd catch a break. I ran into class and sat down quickly, still laughing from our bathroom prank.

"Welcome to class, Jake Peterson. Where have you been?" Mr. Lopez asked.

"Sorry sir," I said. "I was in the bathroom."

Some students laughed, but I was being honest.

"Please try to be on time—that's an important thing to remember throughout your life."

We were three weeks into the school year--I guess this is when teachers get a little more serious. Mr. Lopez's class was all seniors, so he tried to teach us things like punctuality that would help us with jobs in the future, not just teach about current events and cultures.

"Today, we're continuing our discussion about the tragedies that happened this year and how they affected people around the world," Lopez said. "Let's start with a recap of the major tragedies of the year. By 'major' I mean anything that's killed over 10,000 people."

"The Venezuela famine," said Brittany Andrews.

"Right. What was the estimated death toll?"

No answer.

"Roughly," Mr. Lopez said getting impatient.

"Over five million people," Brittany said.

"Right. That's over 20% of their total population. Very tragic. And it is still going on. What's another tragic event that's happened this year?"

"The Middle East wars," someone said from the back of the room.

"Yes. And the death toll so far?"

"Wasn't it 50,000 as of last week?" I said.

"Yes. What else happened this year?"

"Russian wars," said someone from the back of the room.

"Which one?" Chandler asked.

"Why is it that Russia goes to war with another country every year?" asked Brittany.

"While Russia has started wars with many of their neighboring countries, and they are devastating, no single war they've started recently has resulted in over 10,000 deaths," Mr. Lopez said. "What has caused massive casualties over 10,000?"

"The earthquakes in Chile and Bolivia," said Amber Wilcox.

"Right," Lopez said. "Do you remember the death toll?"

"Ah, I think like 300,000 people," Amber said.

"Actually, it was over half a million," Mr. Lopez said. "So why are all of these things happening and what impact does that have on the world? Not just the impact in the areas that had the devastation, but on everyone worldwide?"

"It means the world is coming to an end very soon," Hunter Tate said.

There was some laughter from a few students.

"OK, some people believe that is exactly what's happening," Lopez said.

"It's true," he said.

Hunter was a sackcloth, so it's no surprise he said that. Sackcloths were a group of Christians that wore a piece of burlap as a sign to God that they were repentant. They believe the end of the world is coming soon and that the sackcloth was a sign that will make Jesus's destruction pass by them when He comes again.

Sackcloth and ashes were taught in the Bible. In the Old Testament, after Jonah was spit out of the whale, he went to the people of Nineveh to preach repentance. As a result of his preaching, the people wore sackcloth and sat in ashes to demonstrate to God that they were sorry for their sins. Sackcloth is woven material like the sacks that potatoes are in.

Hunter wore a piece of burlap as a belt. At my school, Sackcloths wore burlap or some woven fabric as a belt, scarf, vest or just tied on a belt loop or purse. It's a sign just like a Jewish person wears a yamaka to show that they are a devout Jew.

Hunter Tate told everyone in class that the end of the world was coming very soon and that every disaster was predicted in the Bible, so we'd better prepare for the end.

"I respect his opinion," said Selena Sanchez. "But we've been having disasters for decades, and just because there may have been more of them this year does not mean the world is going to end."

"What does everyone think?" Mr. Lopez asked to get the discussion going.

"I agree with Selena," said Amber. "Just because more disasters are happening does not mean this is the end of the world. What does 'the end of the world' mean anyway? Do you believe everyone will die tragically?"

"No. The Bible says the earth will be cleansed with fire before the Second Coming of Jesus Christ," Hunter said.

"I'm with Hunter," said my best friend Chandler. "I think these are signs of the times, but I'm also not sure if the end is coming really soon."

"I sure hope not," I said, "because I want to graduate first!"

The class laughed.

We talked in detail about what the end of the world means. There were many different opinions. Some people believed the destruction was a sure sign from God. Others thought it was just bad luck. And some people had no opinion at all.

There were some kids who were really afraid and worried.

I was raised in a good Christian family—not just Easter and Christmas Christians, but the kind that attends church weekly and discusses God often at home. Given that background, I feel like the end is near. There have been too many signs that were straight from the Bible, so I thought there was a strong possibility.

Sometimes people refer to the Second Coming of Christ as the end of the world because of all the destruction that's supposed to happen. But I don't let the possibility of more destruction or the end of the world get me down. I believe life is meant to be lived happily—not in fear of what might happen.

My parents—Tom and Melissa Peterson— taught me to put things into an eternal perspective. They taught me to be prepared for anything, to be kind to everyone regardless of differences, and to help everyone—especially when times are tough. But there are some people who get bothered and angry about everything. People on both sides of the political spectrum seem to always be at each other's throats. I couldn't live like that. People are more important than politics.

The extremists seem to all be in my debate class. Maybe that's why it's been my favorite class this year. Extremists oppose everyone that doesn't believe the way they do. With some people, you have to walk on eggshells around them because they get so easily offended by everything. Life's too short for that. Too short to be angry or violent. If something is wrong, try to change it. But with certain issues, there is no clear right and wrong and you must agree to disagree. If you let the opinions of others bother you, you may struggle with being happy.

Other people play the blame game—blaming anyone for their situation –government, parents, teachers, even God. You never win that game, and I don't think those people can be truly happy either.

True happiness comes from within and is independent of what's happening around you.

This week in debate class, Ms. Vollmer was having us debate a tough subject. She picked the topic of whether violence and anger were effective negotiation tools. She asked if anger and violent protests were the way to change laws in our country. We had to take sides on why we should or shouldn't use violence to change a law.

I was on the side that supported not using violence as a tool to influence government officials. The negative side. That was easy because I supported that stance completely. In our first proposition, we mentioned the fact that there is already too much anger in the world today, and that anger leads to violence, which leads to fighting, revenge and even killings. We talked about anger being a tool that drives a wedge between citizens and ruins our unity.

The opposition by the affirmative group—those in favor of using violence and anger—said that sometimes government officials don't see the urgency of an issue without the use of anger. They felt that if anger can wake up politicians and get them to change out-dated laws, then the violence was justified—it was a means to an end, and any death or destruction caused along the way was merely collateral damage.

Today's class was closing arguments. I gave the rebuttal for my group. I focused on three primary issues. First, anger is bad for your health. It's been proven to cause anxiety and increase your risk of heart attack and stroke. I related good health to happiness and said that in the end, everyone wants to be happy. Second, anger can escalate quickly into violence or force. When people use force or threaten with guns or violence, it causes further fractions in our society. A society that can act civilly while co-existing with their differences is a sophisticated society destined for happiness and success. And third, there already exists a process for laws to be changed that does not require anger or force. Anger and force don't change laws. They just show how you feel, but they don't change anything. By using anger and violence, we further divide this country.

The affirmation group's rebuttal was focused on changing laws. Our school historian, Susan Johnson, was their group's presenter. She's an EDM, which stands for "eat, drink and be merry." EDM's are people who party, drink and/or do drugs often. Some of them have even come to school drunk or high.

In the Bible, there's a scripture that says "eat, drink and be merry, for tomorrow we die." The philosophy of EDM's is "if the world's coming to an end, I want to enjoy every last minute of it." That's ok if they did a lot of good things, too, but they make party-ing priority number 1 over family, friends, homework, and helping others. Most of them just don't care about much. That bothers me. I don't think it's ever worth it to give up or stop doing good things. Especially now…

Like any class of people, some EDM's are extreme, and some are not so extreme. The hardcore ones are not usually the type of people that have a lot of substance to them. It's probably the effect of all the drugs. Many are addicted to alcohol or drugs. They feel that as long as they are not hurting anyone else, they should be able to do whatever they want. But they don't realize that they are often hurting themselves, and by doing that, they are hurting people around them.

There are several EDM's in my school but not necessarily extreme ones. It's an easy life. You don't have to do much to fit in. EDM's invite everyone to their parties, but I don't go to many of them because I don't drink or take drugs.

I made a commitment never to drink after my grandparents were killed by a drunk driver when I was 12 years old. The drunk guy who hit them was in a huge SUV, ran a red light and T-boned them. Their small car was demolished, and their bodies so badly destroyed that they had closed caskets at their funeral. My parents taught me about the dangers of drinking after my grandparents died and taught me how bad it was to drink and drive. Throughout my teenage years, I associated drinking with the death of my grandparents. For that reason, I have not wanted to drink, and I even have a little anxiety when others drink around me.

At the time in my life when everyone seems to want to try adult things like drinking, I've decided it is not for me. Ever. I know that's odd, but that's who I am and my friends respect that.

I don't think Susan Johnson is an extreme EDM. But she's well-known around school as a heavy partier.

Susan's argument focused on laws that were discriminating. She said that America should not discriminate and any law that needs to be changed should be done swiftly and with any force needed to make sure America stops all discrimination.

Anything that could offend anyone offended Susan Johnson. She's the type that felt violent protests were the way to solve every issue. If she wanted the city to put in a new streetlight, she'd probably protest until it happened. She'd stage a violent protest to fight against violence. In my mind, that's like drinking to promote sobriety or sleeping around to promote virginity.

Susan was a pretty, blonde hair, blue-eyed girl. Tall and popular. That gave her confidence. She positioned most government officials as old and out-of-touch people, not eager to change laws that allow all Americans to do whatever they want. "If that means we need to use anger and disorder to ensure that law makers get the point and change laws that discriminate, it is worth the effort to be angry and violent," she said.

There were some cheers from their group after Susan finished.

"Well done to both groups," Ms. Vollmer said. "I will announce the winners on Monday."

I'm sure Susan Johnson thought she beat my team, but Ms. Vollmer was a peacemaker and against fighting, so as long as our points were well presented, we should win this one.

"Also, next week we will be debating China's new law using abortion to stop their over-crowded population problem," she said.

We can't wait for that one. Every week our debate topics get more intense. Kind of like our world today.

CHAPTER 2

THE CONDITION
OF THE WORLD

After a month into the new school year, I was more aware of problems in the world than ever before, thanks to my world events class and debate class. I've learned about disasters, conflicts, fighting and more.

I understand that people want to fight when something is morally or ethically wrong. But when it's merely a different way of doing something, those opinions should not cause such an outrage of anger or fighting. Just because someone believes differently than you, doesn't mean they need to change. Different opinions should be able to exist in society.

But even in America, some people don't accept any differences, and they feel that everyone who doesn't believe the way they believe is wrong. I think Ms. Vollmer's debate class has already helped a lot of students to understand and accept differences.

On Monday, we were excited to go to debate class to find out who won last week's project.

"Last week's winning debate team was the team supporting non-violence," Ms. Vollmer said.

Equal amounts of cheers and boos were heard in the room.

Ms. Vollmer was a relatively new teacher at our school. She was a short, slender woman with long sandy blonde hair from the Midwest. Friendly enough, but definitely in charge of the classroom. She was an expert debater and one of my favorite teachers.

"Now for this week's assignment," she said. "I'm handing out an overview of China's new abortion policy. I've also included a sheet of paper that lists the teams who are going to debate for this policy and those who are debating against it."

"I want everyone to read their outlines first, then you can ask questions as a group," she said. "After that, we'll break into teams. Let's have the pro-abortion group use the back half of the room and the pro-life group use the front half," she continued.

I got my handouts and quickly looked at the list, hoping Ms. Vollmer would know me enough to put me on the team fighting against abortion.

I looked at the list and found my name. "PRO" it said by my name. I had to convince others that abortion was a good thing. I can't do that.

"Ms. Vollmer," I said raising my hand and trying to be polite.

"Yes?" she said.

"I really can't debate why China should allow abortions. I'm so against that."

"I know Jake," Vollmer said. "But remember I'm not asking you to change your opinion, I'm only asking you to pretend like you're China and present your solution for your population problem."

"But Ms. Vollmer, could I please join the other team on this one? This is a major issue for me."

"Jake, learning how to present both sides helps your ability to debate in college and with your future job. When you understand both sides of a point, you can more strategically present points to expose the issues with the other side and win any debate."

"But–"

"I've made the teams, and I'm sticking with them."

I was devastated. It was only a high school debate, but asking me to convince people that China should use abortion to control its overpopulation problem was like saying it was ok to kill your little sister. It was so wrong to me.

Begrudgingly, I sat back in my chair feeling defeated.

After a few minutes, Vollmer asked, "Does anyone have any questions before we break into groups?"

I went to my group and we worked on a plan. I had Chandler and Tyson in my group, plus Susan and a bunch of other talented people. Susan was the most pro-choice one in our group, so this was easy for her. Most of the rest of us were either neutral or pro-life.

Our group focused on the fact that either way, people in China would die. The overpopulation problem would cause hunger issues and potentially mass deaths and disease. Either the Chinese would die from running out of food or from abortion. As much as I was against this policy, the reasoning made sense.

But thinking of what Ms. Vollmer said, we knew we had to be able to rebut what the other team would say—that murder is murder... and it is wrong.

We focused on the fact that China is not a free country—it is communist, and, in those countries, the government makes the laws, not the people. In China, society's moral values don't come before communist law.

Surprisingly, we had the grounds for a great debate in favor of something that I was still totally against. But it taught me how people can be swayed to believe in something because of how it's presented. I think that's how people who support abortion can feel good about it—because it's presented as a woman's right to choose, not a woman's right to kill.

If I were on the other team, I'd bring up that there are other ways to solve over-crowding, like giving free birth control, doing more to eliminate poverty, sex education and more. Over-crowding in general could be aided by building new communities in remote, rural parts of China. Building cities where there aren't any is a better solution than allowing the population to mushroom out of control to the point where starvation kills millions.

There's always a good way to accomplish things. It doesn't involve doing something drastic, and sometimes it isn't the easiest plan. What is right is not always what is easy. Sometimes doing the right thing requires extra thought and effort. But it's worth it.

As we talked, I zoned out thinking that America has its share of issues. The best word to describe people today is "divided." Republican and Democrat politicians hate each other and are angry about everything the other party does. They twist each other's words to raise doubts in the minds of voters.

Special interest groups fight against the government and each other. It is the ultimate irony—fighting for peace and unity. The only people who seem happy are those who don't get caught up in the politics—which luckily is many of the people in our high school.

If you dwell on all the bad things, life is terrible and dangerous. But there is still a lot of good in our country. Your outlook on life is solely determined by whether you focus on the good or the bad. There are still a lot of freedoms in America. And I wouldn't live anywhere else.

CHAPTER 3

KATIE MARTIN

One day between classes, a group of radical sackcloths had a smaller kid cornered in the hall by the auditorium.

Extreme sackcloths believe that it's their responsibility to punish sinners and this kid had just come out as gay—something they didn't agree with.

I walked onto the scene when the punching started.

As I approached, I said in a deep voice "Hey, what's going on?" as if I were a teacher.

That startled them enough that they stopped for a moment—a good element of surprise in any fight.

I stood between the kid and the sackcloths and said, "What's the crime, guys?"

"He's come out as gay," said the biggest one of them. The leader was a senior guy named Gary. I remember him as a freshman, and he was a quiet sackcloth back then. Not sure when he changed. He had a scruffy beard and dressed in black with a piece of sackcloth tied to his belt loop.

"The Bible says its wrong," said another one of the sackcloths.

"But who gave you the right to enforce the Bible?" I asked.

"This doesn't concern you Peterson," Gary said.

But I persisted. "The Bible also says to love one another, so if you hurt this kid, you are breaking the commandments of the Bible which is the compass for your life."

They gave me that look of not wanting to hear what I said, even though they knew what I said was right. They looked frustrated with me.

Getting closer to the sackcloths, I said "Guys, think this through. If you beat him up, you'll be offending the same God who you say you follow. Of all people, surely *you* don't want to offend God, do you?"

I'm not sure where that came from, but it worked, and they slowly walked away.

"Thanks," said the kid who was saved from a beating.

"No worries man. Be careful. What's your name?"

"Michael Davis."

"Michael, I'm Jake–"

"I know who you are," he said. "Thanks again for helping me."

In the middle of all of this, a senior girl had walked by. Katie Martin. Nearly every guy considers her to be the prettiest girl in the whole school. She was a beautiful brunette with blue eyes and a gorgeous smile. We knew each other by name but weren't really friends. And we didn't have any classes together or even the same lunch hour.

I think she was a good Christian, but I heard she was also part of the EDM party crowd at times too. I don't think she's a big Eat, Drink & Be Merry type of person—that doesn't seem like her true character.

As she approached, she noticed me helping Michael. Then as she passed by, she looked at me with a big grin on her face.

I guess when she saw me helping Michael, it wasn't the first time she had seen me helping someone. But for some reason, when she saw me helping him today, she felt a connection to me.

Attraction makes people do funny things. In this case, she went out of her way to find me after school that day. She first sat in the bleachers watching football practice.

After practice and a shower, I headed to my car to find her standing by it talking on her phone. When she saw me, she quickly got off the call.

I was tired from practice but excited to see her. I always wondered if she was more than eye candy, and perhaps this was my chance to find out.

"Hi," she said with great enthusiasm.

"Hey," I said, trying to be cool. "What's up?"

"I wanted to thank you for helping that kid that the radicals were trying to beat up today. That was so nice of you…. And a very brave thing to do."

"Oh. It was nothing. Michael would have done the same thing for me," I said, trying to be humble.

"He would have gotten beat up without you," she said in a laugh. "Why do you help people?"

"I just feel like everyone needs a friend, and sometimes people need a little extra help when they're having a bad day."

"You are too nice of a guy."

"Nah."

"We should hang out sometime," she said with a big smile.

"I'm going to grab some dinner right now. Do you want to join me?" I was expected home for dinner, but I really wanted to hang out with her, and I'm sure my parents would understand.

"Absolutely," she said.

I opened the car door for her and invited her in. She looked at me as if no one had ever done that for her before.

"Thank you," she said. "Such a gentlemen."

I hurried around the car and got in.

"Are we ready for East High on Friday?" she asked.

"They are beatable if we can keep pressure on their quarterback. He's good, but if we keep hitting him, we should be able to win."

"You like to hit people? That seems ironic after watching you protect that freshman boy," she said jokingly.

I laughed, mesmerized by her smile. How did she look so gorgeous all the time?

"Are you ok with Greek food?" I said, knowing that I couldn't take a classy girl like Katie Martin to a fast-food place.

"Of course. I'm good with any food."

I believed her, knowing that someone of her family's financial status likely ate out often and at nicer places. I knew she was cultured, so I wanted to go somewhere she'd appreciate.

"So why do you think those radical sackcloths can't leave people alone?" she said.

"I don't know why they make it their business to be involved in everyone else's business," I said.

"It's been bad for our school. It causes a major division with everyone, and I don't like it," she said.

"Hey, you're the senior class president—what are you doing about it?"

"Can we do anything to solve it? I'm not sure how you change the character of a person. That needs to come from within," I said.

"Well Jake Peterson, are you an intellectual? I thought you were just a handsome football player..."

I just smiled, not expecting that comment from her.

We arrived at the Greek restaurant, and I was amazed at how easy she was to talk with. We got along so well. I had dated a few girls before, but it was usually a one-time date like homecoming, prom, or some unique event.

I wasn't opposed to dating; I just didn't want to get serious unless I really liked the girl. I didn't need a girlfriend just to have a girlfriend, like my friend Tyson. Tyson always has to have a girlfriend. I didn't want to lead anyone on.

We were seated in a quiet booth, and the restaurant was almost empty—which wasn't a surprise on a Wednesday night. That made it seem like it was our private restaurant for the night.

"I should probably text my parents and let them know where I'm at," I said. "They worry about me way too much."

"Mine too," Katie said, texting her parents. "Why do they do that?"

"I think they view society more dangerously than we do," I said. "My parents always talk about how much nicer people used to be."

"Yes, mine too," she said. "I guess we don't know anything different, growing up in the world the way it is today. We've always had a major division between people."

We got along great and quickly had some chemistry between us. We talked about many different things and laughed a lot. Every topic was easy to talk about and we shared the same opinion on almost everything—from politics to school to social issues to the chicken souvlaki we were having.

Before we knew it, it was nine o'clock, and the restaurant was closing. We spent a few hours there, but it seemed like 20 minutes. We should have known it was time to go because both of our parents were texting us to come home.

"I guess I need to take you home," I said.

"If you have to," she said with a laugh.

"You're so easy to talk to."

"You're not so bad yourself," she said.

The ride to her house was more of the same. She and I hit it off so well, I didn't want it to end. She didn't either. She took my phone and entered her info in my contacts. I liked that she took control.

At her house, I met her father in the driveway. Since she texted him with details on when she'd be home, he wasn't upset with her. But he wanted to meet me. Like me, Katie had only been on a few dates, and they were usually for prom or homecoming—not a first date on a school night with a guy that she just got to know during the date.

Meeting adults never scares me—even if I kept their daughter for five hours after school. I've found if you're responsible and respectful, you'll get along with any adult.

"Dad, this is Jake Peterson," she said with a smile.

"Great to meet you," he said with a very firm handshake. He had big strong hands. He was a very distinguished looking man. Tall and handsome for an older man. Katie said he was the owner and CEO of some cool tech company. He seemed friendly, but confident—like someone you want as a friend and didn't want to get on his bad side.

"I'm sorry we're so late, sir," I said. "We just got to talking and didn't realize how late it was."

"That's ok. Thanks for bringing her home safe."

"Dad, Jake's the starting linebacker on the football team and the team captain," Katie said.

"Very cool. Are we going to beat East on Friday night?"

"Yes sir, I think so."

"Get after that quarterback Simmons," he said.

I realized he knew a thing or two about football. Heck, with his build, he could've been a defensive lineman in the NFL.

"That's our plan," I said. "Hit him early and often, coach says."

"Good plan. And contain both edges so he can't scramble."

"Yes sir. Did you play football in school?"

"Dad played at UCLA until an injury ended his chances to go to the NFL," Katie said.

"Really? What position did you play?"

"I was an outside linebacker—an edge rusher in a 3-4 defense."

"I bet that was fun. Sorry about the injury."

"I'll have to come and watch you play on Friday night. I love a good rivalry game."

"That would be great sir. I'll give Simmons an extra hit just for you," I said, trying to connect with him a little more.

"Sounds good. Have a good night," he said as he turned and walked to his door. "Katie, let's go. It's a school night."

"See you tomorrow, Jake Peterson," she said.

"Thank you," I said. "That was fun."

I had never felt before what I felt that night. What started as a simple invitation to dinner turned into a date that I'll always remember. I was surprised at how compatible we were, and that energized me. I was smiling from ear to ear when I got home. My parents were tired from a long day and a little disturbed that I stayed out late on a school night, but once they realized I was safe and didn't have any homework due tomorrow, they were ok.

My mom was interested in the details about Katie Martin, my dad not so much. My mom is the hopeless romantic while my dad was more of a realist—we were two high school kids, and it's rare that high school sweethearts ever end up together.

But mom and I talked about Katie for a while, and she was happy that I had a fun date.

"So, are you going to ask her to the homecoming dance?" mom said.

"Ah, maybe... I guess so, if things keep going well."

"Well, you have a few weeks to think about it," she said. "I can't wait to meet her."

"You'd love her mom. She is pretty, smart and kind."

My friends were texting me all night to get the details on my date because they saw her waiting for me after practice. I just told them she was a blast, and I'd talk with them in the morning. Guys always want details, hoping to hear something juicy.

The next morning at the football team weightlifting practice before school, the guys were giving me a hard time about going out with her so suddenly.

"You don't even know her, and you took her to dinner?" Ben said.

"Sounds like something Tyson would do!" Chandler said.

"Hey, watch it," said Tyson.

"But really, how was she?" Ben said. "What happened?"

Chandler Smith, Tyson Jenson, and Ben Taylor were my three best friends. We played football together, had most classes together, and all were on student council together.

I told them everything—how cool she was, how well we hit it off, and that we talked constantly about everything.

"Any lip action?" Chandler said?

"Not yet," I replied. "But soon, I'm sure," I laughed.

They harassed me throughout weightlifting practice, but I didn't care. I wanted to see Katie again and I knew she wanted to see me too. I had never connected with a girl as quickly as I did with Katie.

During school, I didn't see Katie until after fourth period. She was walking down the hall with her three BFF's. Katie hung out with Susan Johnson, Sarah Adams, and Kellie Roberts. They were quite the group: Susan and Sarah, Kellie, and Katie. Their names even went together well. All four of them lived on the same street and all are very popular girls.

Her friend Susan Johnson, from my debate class, lived next door to Katie and threw a lot of parties at her house. I don't know if Katie felt pressured to party; I'd like to think she did what she wanted to do when she wanted to do it. But when all your best friends are partying all the time, it's possible that eventually you're likely to feel you need to do it in order to fit in.

"Jake Peterson!" she said. I loved it that she called me by first and last name.

"Hey, how's it going?" I asked.

"I had a wonderful time last night," she said. "And my dad likes you—that's a first."

"Oh good. He seems really cool."

"Yes, he is. He hasn't liked most guys I've brought to the house, so that's a good sign."

As we talked, everything around us seemed to fade away. Katie's friends went to class without her. Before we knew it, the bell rang, and we were both late to class. That was okay for me because I had student council and could be late.

But Katie had Mr. Stevenson for biology next period, and he was a jerk to people who were late. He started class the second after the bell rang every day. He always said, "I don't make you wait for me, so don't make me wait for you."

"Stevenson is going to kill me," Katie said.

She needed help so she wouldn't get in trouble with Stevenson. I had him last year and survived it, but he was rough. When you get on his bad side, he doesn't let you live it down for the rest of the year.

So, I decided to step in and help her out. Luckily, Stevenson liked me, or at least, respected me because I respected him.

"I have an idea," I said. "Just go along with me for a bit."

"What are you going to do?"

I walked with her to Stevenson's class and told Mr. Stevenson that I needed Katie for a student council project. I told him I had filled out paperwork for her to be dismissed from class today, but "my assistant lost it" before it was submitted.

"Your assistant?" Stevenson asked.

"My assistant in student council," I said. "But since the paperwork was not submitted properly, Katie suggested that she come to your class and offered to assist us in student council another time."

I was trying to make her look good with Stevenson—like she wanted to attend his class. *No one* wanted to attend his class!

"So, I made her late because we were talking in the hall about this student council project," I said. "It's my fault. I'm sorry for that, and I'm bringing her to you."

"Well, ok," Stevenson said, hesitantly. "Thank you. When you get the paperwork submitted, then you can take her for your little project."

I got her off the hook for being late. It was one of those benefits of being senior class president—teachers trusted me.

She silently said "thank you," as she took her seat.

I didn't see her the rest of that day, but we texted that night. She initiated it, which was cool.

"How was your day?" she texted.

"Long," I texted. *"And yours?"*

"Same. My friends are calling me 'Jake's little project," she texted.

"LOL. That's funny," I texted.

"Maybe for you!" she replied.

We didn't get into much of a discussion because we both had a lot of homework. But she kept joking about being my little project.

Thank you, Mr. Stevenson!

I told her any time she needed to get out of any class, I'd be happy to help.

But I needed to get my mind on track for tomorrow night's game. So, I cut it short and wished her a good night so I could finish homework and get to bed… even though I didn't want to.

CHAPTER 4

EXPECTING THE UNEXPECTED

F riday was game day, and we had a spirit assembly scheduled at the end of the day because of the rivalry with East High. We only have a couple spirit assemblies all season. They were fun and a good excuse to get out of class.

It was our third game of the season, and we wanted to stay undefeated. From the start of the season, we were ranked to win our conference, so there has been a lot of pressure on us. We won our first two games easily, but East would be more of a challenge.

When everyone heard about the preseason rankings at the beginning of the school year, their expectations of us were set very high. That can cause some guys to feel pressure. But pressure is what you make of it. I don't let it build up inside me. Too many guys let it get the best of them and then they make mistakes. But we were planning to make the prediction right and win our conference.

The spirit assembly was the last period of the day, so students were already excited to be done for the week. And football Fridays are even more exciting.

The players stayed in the locker room waiting for all students and teachers to get seated in the gym. Once everyone was seated, we were to run in on coach's signal and line up in the center of the gym. Even though it wasn't a game, it had the excitement of one.

"You nervous, man?" asked Chandler as we waited in the locker room.

"No. Just excited for tonight," I said. "We have to beat them."

"Dude, you and me are going to be a two-man wrecking crew tonight," he said.

"That's my plan" I said, giving him a high five.

"OK, let's go!" yelled coach.

We were all yelling as we ran out. Chandler and I were near the back of the line of players.

There was a bottle neck through the door as there were a lot of students and teachers right outside the locker room door, so our team had to run almost single file through everyone.

As I got through the door, I heard a voice I had hadn't heard all day.

"Hey Jake Peterson!" Katie was in the group of students right outside the door.

I went from a run to a jog-in-place so I could talk to her for just a second. "Hey. You're coming to the game tonight, right?"

"Of course," she said looking at me with those gorgeous blue eyes.

"Will you do something for me?" she asked.

"What's that?" I said, stopping.

"Will you sack that quarterback tonight?" she said. "For me."

"You bet I will."

Every other player ran past me. Then came the coaches.

"Peterson, we need to get on the court!" my coach said.

"I'm on my way." "Katie, I gotta run."

"I'll be watching you, number 50."

I wore number 50 all four years of high school. It was my thing. In the history of the NFL, there have been some great linebackers who wore #50. I wanted to set a high standard for my play by picking that number as a freshman.

Chandler and Tyson met me at center court to give me crap.

"Dude, is Katie going to be a distraction to your game?" Chandler said with a laugh.

"We need you tonight," Tyson said.

"Guys, I'm fine," I said. "If anything, it gives me a little extra energy for the game."

"Whatever you need to motivate you, do it!" Chandler said.

"Maybe you should make out with her before the game," Tyson joked.

"Shut up," I said, punching him in the arm.

The spirit assembly was exciting. Everyone sang the school fight song, and then the cheerleaders did a cheer.

Coach Davidson was up next, and he didn't disappoint. He's a great motivator.

"West View High!" he yelled. "Are you ready?!"

The crowd cheered "yes!"

"Are you ready to beat East High Badgers?!"

"Yes!" the crowd yelled back.

"We are the team who can beat them," he said.

As the crowd calmed down, he calmed down a bit, but he still spoke with great energy. "I want to announce the starters for tonight's game, starting with our offense," coach said. "At quarterback, give a big cheer to senior Bruce McMichaels!"

As he announced players, I looked around the gym at all the posters people made. "Beast beats East!" "Burn the Badgers!" "Bury the Badgers." "Spartans eat Badger Burgers!" Funny stuff.

As I looked around, I looked back toward the locker room to see if I could spot Katie. I was still looking for her when I hear coach say, "Starting middle linebacker and the key to our defense, senior captain Jake Peterson!"

I ran out to the coach, giving a high five to other players on the way and loved hearing the cheers of the crowd. Those cheers never get old.

"Next up, Peterson's partner in crime, starting outside linebacker, senior Chandler Smith!" coach said.

Chandler ran out to a ton of cheers too. He gave me a high five and then gave me a big hug.

"Next is junior Keshawn Jones, who's our other outside linebacker!" coach said.

"You boys ready to kick some butt tonight?" Keshawn asked.

"Definitely!" we shouted.

"Our defensive line is made up of seniors Tim Perry, David Ross, and Ben Taylor and junior Zeke Dew," coach said.

The crowd cheered again.

"Cornerbacks are senior Tyson Jensen and junior Hector Gonzalez," coach said. "And our safeties are senior Brian Milano and junior Octavio Martinez."

As the crowd cheered with a little less gusto, coach got them going again.

"This is YOUR Spartan team!" he yelled. "We're going to win tonight!"

Coach Davidson got the crowd more excited when he started a chant, "Beat East High, Beat East High!" The whole school was yelling it at the top of their lungs. Coach loved the level of excitement for the big game. It was energizing to every member of my team.

After the assembly, I went home to eat and get ready. I have a pre-game ritual that involves loud music, stretching, and making mean faces in the mirror. Don't ask me why. But the mean faces help me envision overpowering an offensive lineman and getting to the quarterback. I feel if I can see it in my mind, it makes it come more naturally. Crazy, I know. Every player has some kind of pre-game ritual... that's what I do.

I drove to school earlier than we were supposed to be there. The game was at seven, and we were supposed to be there by six, but I got there at 5:45. I do a lot of stretching before every game.

When I parked my car, I saw Coach Davidson talking with a reporter outside the locker room. Davidson was a cool guy and a great coach. He was like a second father to me.

Coaches motivate players in different ways. Some yell at their players. Some tell them to prove they deserve to be on the team. Some are quiet. Others pump them up with motivational type quotes. Coach Davidson was not negative with us. He yelled when he needed to, but he'd never put us down. His philosophy was always to build us up and make us feel like we could do anything we set our minds to. I liked that about him.

"Hey coach!" I said.

Coach turned away from the reporter and said, "Jake, my man!" as he gave me a high five.

There weren't always reporters at every game, but East High was a rival, and this was a big game. They had some good athletes, but we knew we could win if we played our game.

I went into the locker room and was the only player there. That's what I wanted. I like getting dressed at my pace and I stretch along the way. I try to be ready by the time all the players arrive so I can pump them up while they're getting ready.

"How are you feeling about tonight?" coach said, returning from his interview.

"I'm ready."

"Just remember what we practiced—you and Chandler team up with each other and alternate the decoy role so the other one can get to Simmons."

"We're excited sir. I think it's a great plan."

Coach went to his office so I could change.

Their quarterback, Brad Simmons, had a great arm, but he wasn't very mobile. So if you could get through his offensive line, you could usually hit him. I respected him but I also wanted to sack him and throw him off his game.

A lot of our students hated Simmons and talked trash about him. But that's just how some people support their team. I approach it as a game. We want to outsmart them and outplay them, but afterwards when the game is over, we should still be friends. No one should be an enemy.

Chandler was next to arrive. "Dude!" he said to me.

"Dude! You ready?"

"Yes I am. I was thinking that this could be the biggest game of our high school careers."

"Definitely. So don't screw it up."

"HA. No worries."

"Let's just remember the decoy strategy so we can both get some sacks tonight!"

Chandler was my best friend. We knew everything about each other. Maybe that's why we were a great linebacking tandem.

More players arrived and were getting ready. I got all dressed and visited with other players to pump them up.

I always go to Bruce McMichael first—the QB.

"Bruce, tonight is your night my man," I said. "I feel something great coming from you tonight!"

"Yes sir! We're going to put up some points tonight!"

Bruce was six foot four—tall for a high school quarterback. That helped him see over the line. He was sort of a hybrid EDM— he partied some, but was disciplined enough to be on the football team. He was a good QB and might have a chance to play at the college level. He had applied to a couple colleges and was waiting to hear back.

"After tonight, USC and UCLA are going to hand you a scholarship," I said.

"Thanks man. I sure hope so."

I hung out with my friends Ben and Tyson, pumping them up too.

"Guys, there's a scout here tonight from the Chargers, so you play your best," I joked.

"Really?" Ben said.

He was the more gullible one.

"Dude, he's just joking with you," Tyson said.

"Oh man, don't do that to me!" Ben said.

"You know the game plan forwards and backwards?" I asked. That was something coach would always ask us.

"Yes coach," they both said mocking me almost in unison, and laughed loudly afterwards.

I went from player to player and position to position. My goal was to let everyone know that I expected us to win. And no matter what happened, we were never to give up. I promised I wouldn't give up and they did too. I did that before every game.

"OK guys, let's go out and warm up in your position groups!" yelled Coach Davidson.

We were to be on the field by 6:30 for 15 minutes, then back to the locker room for our pre-game pep talk.

Pre-game warmups are a ritual in football at every level. In high school, there are two types of players: those who take warmups seriously; and guys who use warmups to show off for the girls.

The girls who are easily impressed by that seem to be hanging around the fence so they can get as close as they can to the field.

Other girls were in the stands. And that's where I saw Katie. She was with her friends. She noticed me looking her way and gave me a little wave.

"Peterson, stay focused!" Chandler yelled.

The linebacker group burst out in laughter.

I refocused on doing my warmups. I needed to keep my head in the game.

When warmups were over, we ran back into the locker room for the pep talk.

"Dude, did you see the way Katie Martin was looking at you?" Chandler said, as we were running into the locker room.

"She wasn't looking at Jake, she was looking at me," said Tyson.

Tyson was the lady killer. He thought every girl in school liked him... and they probably did. He was a good-looking guy that could turn on the charm with the ladies.

"All right guys," coach said. "Let's settle down. We've been preparing for this game since the season started. From two-a-days in the heat of summer, to our first two games—all of this has been preparation for tonight."

"Yes sir," several players said.

"The key tonight is to remember your assignments. Don't change the strategy. And don't get down. We have to believe we're going to win. They might score first. Heck, they may be winning by two touchdowns in the fourth quarter, but don't any of you give up. Each one of you must believe we can win this. I believe it. Do you?"

"Yes!" we all said loudly. Then a cheer broke out spontaneously: "Yes, yes, yes..."

"OK, let's go out there and win this thing!"

"Yeah," all the guys said as we got up, put on our helmets, and headed toward the doors.

"Wait here until I give you the signal," said Mr. Lopez, our assistant coach. A few seconds passed and then, "OK—GO!"

We ran out the door through two rows of cheerleaders and broke through a paper banner that read "BEAST THE EAST!" The crowd went wild.

After a few minutes of lining up on our sidelines and last-minute discussions per positions, we were ready to go. I saw my family in the stands and waved at them. They came to every game. Families of players got to sit in the first four rows of the stands so they could be close to their boys. Sometimes, that wasn't a good thing, especially when a dad yelled at his son to do certain things. But with my family, it was great.

"Everyone please rise and please join together in singing our national anthem," said the woman over the PA system.

We took our helmets off and sang, as we looked at the flag. Our national anthem always gave me the chills. Sure, there were a lot of problems in our country, but there are problems in every country. We are free in America and that was something to be both grateful for and proud of.

Next was the coin toss. Chandler and I were captains tonight, so we both went out to the middle of the 50-yard line for the coin toss. East's captains were their QB Simmons, and another player I didn't know.

"Hey Brad. Good luck tonight."

"You too man," he said.

I found it funny that he was wishing me good luck, since "luck" for me was driving him into the ground.

I didn't know his teammate, so I introduced myself. "Hey, I'm Jake Peterson. What's your name?"

"My name is evil, and you're going to taste death tonight," he said trying to be intimidating. He wore #58 and was their starting middle linebacker.

"None of that," said the official.

"Yeah, I gave up death for Lent," Chandler joked.

"Enough guys," said the official.

"Keep this clean tonight, guys," the official said. "Tell your teammates we won't put up with any cheap shots. Got it?"

"Yes sir," we all said.

"Here's the coin," he said. "This side is heads, and this side is tails. East High, you're the visitors, so you call it in the air." He flipped the coin up.

"Heads," said Simmons.

"It is tails," the official said. "West View High, do you want to start on offense or defense?"

"Offense," Chandler said. Coach always wanted to start on offense so our guys could try to get into a rhythm quickly and hopefully score first.

We ran back to the sidelines and took our spot there while we waited for our offense to do their job.

Every game starts with the players a bit nervous at first. Jitters are a real thing. McMichaels though was as cool as ice. On our first series, he drove 65 yards and scored a touchdown, on six quick plays. He capped it off by running into the end zone on a bootleg fake from the 4-yard line.

Everyone cheered and gave high-fives. As McMichaels came back to the sidelines, I said, "Mr. USC!"

"Thanks Peterson," he said.

Our defense had our share of jitters, missing some easy tackles and letting them move the ball on a couple back-to-back plays.

But soon we settled down and got into the game. We stopped them on a third and long, so our offense got the ball back.

The score stayed 7-0 for the first quarter and part of the second. I was making some tackles but couldn't get to the quarterback.

I was frustrated. It was loud in the stadium, but I swore I heard Katie yelling "Sack him for me, Jake Peterson!" That motivated me.

Before East's next play, I told our defensive backs to stick to their receivers so the quarterback couldn't throw it quickly. Chandler was going to decoy for me—he blitzes long enough to get their defense to focus on him, then I run in from the other side and go after Simmons.

Simmons hiked the ball, Chandler faked the blitz on the left side, and their line bought it, pulling players toward him to block him. That left an opening between the guard and tackle, and I jumped through, got to Simmons, and slammed him to the ground. The crowd went wild.

I pointed up to Katie in the stands to let her know that was for her. It was a rush. She pointed back at me as she cheered.

That one was so much fun, I did it again right before half time. We were up 21-7 at half-time and looking like we were going to win this. Coaches went over game plans. My plan was to get Simmons again. The more we hit him, the more careless he'd be with his passes.

We came out of the locker room to Katie yelling "Let's go Jake Peterson! Let's go number 50!" I was already motivated, but that helped even more.

Our first series on defense, I did the fake blitz to get their line to focus on me, then Chandler pounded through the left side of their line and sacked Simmons too.

"YES!" Chandler shouted.

"Dude, you rock!" I said.

"We got this. Let's keep putting the pressure on them," Chandler said to everyone.

The pressure worked. Simmons was pressured on most plays and sacked four times. It made him nervous in the pocket, which made him throw off target. That's exactly what we wanted to do.

We dominated in the second half and were up 35 – 7 midway through the 4th quarter. Coach pulled starters to keep us from getting injured. I wanted to play. I loved playing. But I also respected my coaches and would sit because they told me to.

Final score was 38-14. We expected to win. We didn't expect to dominate as much as we did. Beating your rival is always important. It sets the tone for the rest of the season and gives us confidence going into the next week.

After the game, we shook hands with the other team. Some guys like to use the handshake as a time to trash talk other players. We don't stoop to that level. This is about sportsmanship, and even if all the players at East High didn't show it, we showed it. I admire that about our team.

I went out of my way to find Evil—their captain, #58.

"Hey 58—you got mad skills, man," I said.

"Shut up," he growled back at me. "You guys got lucky tonight."

"You played a really good game," I said trying to shake his hand.

But #58 just slapped my hand away and went by me. Maybe that's part of being evil, I thought.

I congratulated their coaches too. Their team played well. Yes, they lost, but they did a lot of good things tonight. We all know how hard it is to lose, so I felt I could help soften the blow a bit.

We ran into the locker room for an overview from coach. He was pumped up. We all were. That was a great game.

After that, we all showered and got dressed.

"What are we doing tonight?" Chandler asked.

"I was hoping to take Katie out," I said.

"And just like that, your friendship is over," Ben joked.

"No way man," I said. "Let's all get ice cream at Nielsons tonight. You guys bring as many cheerleaders as you can, and I'll bring Katie, and we'll see you there."

"Sounds like a plan," Chandler said.

CHAPTER 5

QUESTIONS

As soon as I came out of the locker room, I had a local reporter in my face with a microphone who wanted an interview. I was fine with that, although it's the team that won the game and not me.

"Jake, I'm Frank Harrington from the Post. How did it feel to get two sacks on Simmons?"

"Great. We tried to wear him down all night."

"Was the strategy to control Simmons and let other players beat you?" he asked.

"We didn't want any of their players to beat us, but controlling Simmons was our main priority."

"What do you think of your preseason #1 ranking? Is West View High School worthy of that?"

"Well, I don't know for sure, but we played well as a team tonight," I said noticing Katie waiting for me.

After seeing her, I don't remember what else he asked me, or what I said. But when the interview was over, she ran up to me and gave me a hug.

"Great game Jake Peterson! And thanks for giving me two sacks!"

"Oh, the second one wasn't for you," I joked.

"What?"

"That was for your dad."

"Hey!" she said.

"Wanna get out of here?"

"Of course. Let's go."

I loved game nights. But I wanted to spend more time with her.

We walked down the field toward the gate, taking in the aftermath of an exciting game.

"You played so well," Katie said.

"Thank you. It was a great team effort!"

I saw my parents waiting for me by the gate with my little brother and sister. "Come meet my parents," I said.

"Great game son," my dad said.

"Yes, you were awesome," Mom said.

"Thanks. Mom and Dad, this is Katie Martin."

"Hi Katie. So great to meet you," my mom said.

"Nice to meet you as well," Katie said shaking their hands. "I've heard so much about you."

"And this is my little sister Jane. She's 12. And my brother Zack is 10," I said.

"Great to meet you both," Katie said.

"She's so pretty," Jane whispered louder than she thought.

"Oh, thank you," Katie said with a smile.

Jane's face got bright red with embarrassment when she realized Katie heard her.

"We're going to go to Nielsons and get some ice cream with some of the players, ok?"

"That's fine, but don't be too late," mom said.

"We won't."

With that, I took Katie's hand and we walked quickly through the parking lot to my car. Perhaps it was a bit forward to hold her hand already, but it just seemed natural.

When we got to my car, I opened her door and she paused and looked me in the eyes.

"What?" I asked.

"You really are such a gentleman," she said.

"My parents taught me that."

"They seem like great people."

"They are. They've made me who I am today."

"You don't think Mr. Stevenson's biology class had something to do with the man you are today?" she joked.

"Ha. Not even!"

Quickly the chemistry between us grew like when we went to the Greek restaurant earlier this week.

Nielson's Ice Cream was the local gourmet ice cream, custard, and frozen yogurt joint. It's where everyone in high school hung out, especially on weekends.

As we walked in, I was greeted by many students, players, and cheerleaders.

They all complemented me on a great game, but I always give credit to the whole team. When the whole team does their job, everyone shines. I have a hard time taking a direct complement when I know that so many guys performed well tonight.

Chandler, Ben, and Tyson were in the middle of the restaurant, having pushed four tables together because they did bring almost every cheerleader tonight.

"There's the guys," I said, giving them a wave.

"Dude!" Chandler said running over to me in line. "We already ordered. After you order, come sit with us. We saved two seats."

"How's Jake's little project doing tonight?" Chandler asked, hugging Katie.

"Great sack tonight, Chandler," Katie said, avoiding the question.

"Thank you. Couldn't have done it without my wingman, Jake Peterson," he said, as he walked walking back to his table.

The place was packed. It was an old-fashioned ice cream place with black and white checkered flooring, white tables, and red vinyl chairs. The walls were just white. And that was the décor. No one came for the décor. They just came for the ice cream.

"So, what's it feel like to sack a quarterback?" Katie asked, as we waited in a line that wasn't moving.

"It's the best. It's our goal on every play, and it doesn't happen very often, so when you get the sack, it's a huge adrenalin rush, a big celebration."

"Do you think you're going to hit your wife?" she joked. "Jake Peterson, are you going to be a wife beater?"

"No way," I laughed. "I'd never do that!"

"I know. Why do you think some husbands do that?" she asked, getting serious suddenly.

There she goes being philosophical again, I thought. "I have no idea why a guy would hit a girl—married or not. It's so wrong."

We ordered and sat down with the group, but she asked me rapid fire questions the whole time we were at the table. We'd join the conversation with everyone about the game, and then she'd lean over to me and ask something like "Do you like beef or chicken better?" Or "What's your dream car?" Or something more serious like "Is it more important for you to be kind or to be right?"

With each question I answered, I asked her to answer that same question. We both like beef better, would love a Tesla, and felt it's much better to be kind. We seemed to agree on nearly every question she asked.

Even though we sat at a big table of 14 people, Katie and I were in our own little world, talking about various topics through short questions every other minute or so.

After we both answered, we'd join back in with the group talking about school, classes, teachers, and rumors. But after a couple minutes, she'd lean over and ask another get-to-know-you question.

"What's your biggest pet peeve?" she asked.

"People who are mean and unkind," I said.

"Me too."

"Country or rock music?" she asked.

"Definitely rock."

"Same."

"If you won $1 million tomorrow, what's the first thing you'd buy?"

"Hmm. Good question," I said pondering. "I'd probably buy my parents a new house and then I'd buy me a new car. I got the old hand-me-down car from my parents, and it needs a lot of work."

"I thought you were going to say you'd donate it all to charity," she joked.

"Ha," I laughed. "What about you?"

"I'd probably go on a trip to Europe with my friends. I've always wanted to go to Rome and Paris."

"That would be fun. I'd love to visit Europe too."

I was amazed that she and I felt so alike on so many topics. Her questions taught us a lot about each other and showed how much we had in common. Some were serious questions. Some were not.

"Favorite color?" she asked.

"Blue."

"Pink."

"Favorite ice cream flavor?" she asked kind of loudly.

"Definitely chocolate peanut butter."

"Me too!" she said.

"Mine is chocolate chip mint," said Chandler.

Everyone laughed.

"OK, I have one," I said. "Coconut: Love it or hate it?"

"Love it," she said

"What?" I joked. "How could anyone love coconut?"

"That's a relationship killer right there," Chandler yelled from across the table to laughter from the group.

"Well Jake Peterson, I don't know if I can hang out with you anymore if you don't like coconut," she said.

"The feeling is definitely mutual," I said, finishing the last bite of my ice cream.

"Maybe you should just take me home now," Katie said.

"OK."

"Everyone, we're leaving," I announced.

Tyson made kissing sounds and the cheerleader next to him smacked him at first. When he did it again, she leaned into him and kissed him. It started as a funny kiss, but she didn't stop, and it soon became passionate, much to the cheers of everyone at our table.

The cheerleader was Kami Donahoe, a junior that was a big time EDM. She was very pretty with long blonde hair and blue eyes. She was always hanging with the party crowd. I wasn't sure if she really liked Tyson or was just playing, but it was spontaneous and funny.

When we got in the car, I felt such a connection to Katie. It was more than just liking the same foods—other than coconut.

The unexpected was happening with Katie. We were falling for each other. Two people who had no classes together and hardly knew each other until a few nights ago. It was crazy. This wasn't like me.

"It's great how much we talk," I said.

"That's because I'm your little project," she said.

"Yes. My little project."

"What plans do you have for your little project tonight," she asked.

"Well, I need to get you home so you don't miss curfew," I said, trying to be responsible.

"Jake Peterson, do you ever break the rules?!" she asked.

I laughed. "What would you like to do?"

"Well, your little project would like you to come to her house so we can keep talking," Katie said.

"That's the least I could do for my little project," I said.

CHAPTER 6

GETTING CLOSER

Katie lived on the south end of town, along the Avenues. That's where the wealthiest people in our city lived. She drove a Hummer SUV with personalized plates—a present she got for her 17th birthday.

She wasn't necessarily spoiled, but she had everything she wanted. Well, maybe she was spoiled, but she didn't act like it.

At her house I met her mom who looked like she could be Katie's older sister.

"Nice to meet you, Mrs. Martin."

"Oh, call me Hannah," she said. She was a successful Realtor in town, and everyone knew her.

"And good to see you again Mr. Martin."

"Good to see you too. You can call me Jeff. And great game tonight, Jake!"

Jeff and Hannah's house was like something you'd see in an architecture magazine.

Katie was an only child.

"Why didn't you drive your Hummer tonight?" her dad asked.

"Susan gave me a ride tonight," Katie said. "We're going to go in the family room and talk," she said.

"Do you guys want some ice cream?" Hannah asked.

"We just got some with the players and cheerleaders at Nielsons," Katie said.

"But thank you so much," I added.

We went to their family room which was cozy and warm. She turned on the fireplace and we sat on a very comfy couch close to each other.

Her long, dark brown hair looked gorgeous. Her blue eyes seemed to pierce right through me. And her smile was infectious. Katie was so easy to talk to, and I was enjoying every moment with her.

Her question game continued.

"If you were going to be stranded on an island with 1 person, who would it be and why?" she asked.

"Probably Chandler," I said. "He cracks me up and would be very entertaining... how about you?"

"Susan. She's my best friend, and we can talk about anything. If you could only eat one food on that island for the rest of your life, what would it be?"

"Only one for breakfast, lunch and dinner?"

"Yes."

"Is there an oven on the island? Or a BBQ grill?"

"You're overthinking it. What one food could you eat for breakfast, lunch and dinner for the rest of your life?"

"Pizza."

"Pizza?"

"Yes. I'd make a breakfast pizza with eggs and bacon, a lunch pizza, which I guess could be just pizza, and... ah... same with the dinner pizza. And I'd pick a ton of toppings so I could take some off every so often and have a little variety."

"Hmm. Good answer."

"What's yours?"

"Probably steak."

"Just steak? No potatoes or salad with it?"

"Nope—the question was to pick one food" she said. "Ok, next question. What the scariest thing that's ever happened to you?"

The tone of the night just got serious.

"Well, my little brother Zack fell down our stairs, hit his head, and went unconscious when he was five years old. We took him to the hospital. He just had a concussion, but when a little kid gets knocked out, you assume the worst."

"Wow, I can't imagine that. I bet your parents were a wreck, huh?"

"Actually, they were calmer than I think I would be. But they called 911 and paramedics quickly took him to the hospital. Luckily, he only had the concussion—no major brain damage and no broken bones. It was a situation that helped our family bond together."

"I bet. That is scary."

"What's yours, Katie?"

"Last year when I first got my license, I got into a bad accident on the Connector Road and hit a deer. The deer was huge and smashed through my windshield. His antler cut my shoulder a bit. I was bloody, bruised, and traumatized."

"Holy cow! That's crazy. I'm so sorry that happened to you. And it seems like everyone I know who's driven on that road gets in some kind of accident."

In the town of Bonita Del Sol, California, there are two major state highways that go parallel through the city. Katie lives off SR 180 to the south, and I live off SR 67 to the north, closer to the airport. The normal way people get from my end of town to Katie's end of town is by going on Main Street, which connects both state highways. However, a couple of miles before you get to Main Street is Connector Road—a very narrow and dangerous two-lane road that farmers used in the olden days. It's a raised gravel road that has ditches along both sides. There's also a steep hill where many accidents have occurred.

Most people avoid that road because it's hard for two big cars or trucks to pass each other—typically you have to slow down to five mph to make sure you don't hit the other driver or drive off the edge. It's not uncommon to hear of accidents on that road because of how narrow it is. And because there are fields on both sides, there are often deer that cross the road, and it's quite common to see dead deer laying in the road or off in the ditch. There are no lights on the road, making it pitch black at night.

The Bonita Police Department asks any resident who hit a deer to call them, and they will remove the carcass.

"It was so scary," she said. "The deer totaled my car and sent me to the hospital. That's why my parents bought me the Hummer so that I can be safe if it ever happens again. But now I'm not allowed to drive on the Connector even though I have a car that can protect me better. It's kind of ironic."

"Most kids I know have been told not to take that road."

"Yes, almost everyone I know has been told by their parents not to take it."

"Although... you realize it probably cuts about 15 minutes off my drive to your house, so while I know it's a dangerous road, I might just take it if I need to get to your house sooner."

"Jake, don't take the Connector. I'd rather have you get here safely."

"What was going through your head when the deer crashed through your windshield?" I asked. "Did you think you were going to die?"

"It happened so fast that I didn't have time to think. I was driving along and about a second after I saw the deer, it hit me. It was that fast."

"I'm glad you're ok, but I can't imagine how scary that would be."

"Yes. Terrifying. Are you ready for a new question?"

"Where are you getting all these from?" I joked. "But yes, ask away."

"If you could cure one disease, which one would it be and why?"

Another serious question.

"Can I think about that one for a minute?" I asked. "Will you go first?"

"Sure," she said. "I would cure cancer because so many people die from it."

"Good answer," I said. "But that was too fast. I'm still thinking of my answer."

She laughed but looked me in the eyes waiting for my answer. "I didn't think this question would be that tough."

"OK. I have my answer. I would cure the disease of hatred. There are so many people in the world today—heck, even at our school—that have such hatred in their hearts for other people. It's ugly and terrible and is ruining our society. I would put an end to hatred."

"Wow" she said. "I didn't think of hatred as a disease, but I guess it is. That's a great answer. And how do you plan to do that?"

"It's not going to be easy. So often hatred is deeply rooted in people that it's hard to change them. But I think that a couple things need to happen."

"You really have a plan?"

"Well, maybe. I've thought about this a bit. First, we need politicians to work together, like really work together. Every bill that is presented, needs an equal number of each party involved in writing it. That makes it bipartisan before it is introduced. More importantly, neither side would tear it down if both sides worked on it together."

"OK, I like that, if it could work" she said.

"Then, every president has to pick a vice president from the other party," I said.

"Good one, but won't the VP have the president killed so they can become president?" she joked.

"Perhaps," I laughed.

"Then, somehow, people need to change. We need to all realize that before we're Republican or Democrat, before we're for a certain policy or against it, and before we go to this school or that one, or root for this team or that team, everyone needs to remember we are all human beings, and we are all children of God. That must be understood first. From there, we can work toward getting along better and stop being so divided. That doesn't mean we all have to believe the same way—that will never happen. But we need to truly accept differences. I don't know how we do that, but that's what we need to do."

"Ever thought of running for office?" Katie asked.

"Ha, I have thought of what it would be like," I said. "But I don't know if that's my future."

"Jake Peterson, you are going to change the world," she said, putting her head on my shoulder.

"Thank you," I said, realizing how our entire conversation at her house was about serious things.

"It's almost midnight," I said. "I need to get home."

"You have a midnight curfew?" she asked, taking her head off my shoulder.

"Yes. What's your curfew?"

"I don't know that I have one. But I don't often stay out too late."

"That's cool," I said.

"I'll walk you out. My parents are probably in bed, so we need to be quiet through the house."

"OK" I whispered. "Is this quiet enough?" whispering loudly.

Katie laughed. "Yes, that's fine."

"SHHH," I said jokingly.

"Are you shushing me?" she asked with a smile.

"I'd tell you, but I have to be quiet right now," I said laughing, as we walked out her front door.

When we got to my car, I felt an urge to kiss her. In the moonlight, she looked even more beautiful, with her lips glistening from lip gloss and her eyes looking so romantically at me.

"I had a great time tonight," I said. "I love talking with you."

"Yes, it is so cool how connected we are," Katie said.

"I like having you as my little project."

"And I'm happy to be your little project!" she said.

I was looking for signs that she would be ok with a kiss. She was looking me right in the eyes and smiling from ear to ear. I'd say that was my sign.

I think, though, she was wondering the same thing I was: were we ready for this?

Then, taking the opportunity to show me she was ready, she moved toward me slowly. But I couldn't let her take the lead, so I pulled her close to me and kissed her.

It was magical. Warm. And it shot energy through me like I'd never felt before. I didn't want it to end.

As we separated, she smiled even bigger.

"Well Jake Peterson," she said, "you made my night. Thank you for such a great night."

"Thank YOU," I said. "That was so amazing. I had a great time with you."

She watched me as I backed out of her driveway and drove away. Wow. Katie Martin. Who would have thought we'd be together? And after only a few days. But I felt so connected to her.

CHAPTER 7

THE CRAZY WORLD
WE LIVE IN

All weekend I thought about Katie. My family had things planned for me Saturday and Sunday, so she and I mostly texted back and forth.

Tyson texted me, Chandler, and Ben Saturday morning to tell us he made out with that cheerleader—Kami Donahoe—all night Friday.

"You dog!" Chandler texted.

"Congrats man," Ben texted.

I asked if he knew Kami before Friday night.

"I had a class with her last year," Tyson texted.

"Then it's true love!" I said.

"What about you Jake? Did you kiss Katie last night after you left?" Chandler texted.

I didn't want to tell them yet, but I couldn't lie.

"When I kiss Katie as much as Tyson kissed Kami, you guys will be the first to know. I promise!" I texted.

"Cool" Chandler wrote.

"Gotcha" Tyson added.

So, my answer shut them up. For now.

On Monday morning, there was a mass shooting in a factory in Ohio. It was all over the news first thing in the morning. That day in my World Events class we talked about issues of gun violence in America and what to do about it.

"This Ohio shooting was the eighth one of the year," Mr. Lopez said. "These are becoming more and more common. Why?"

"How are people still getting access to semi-automatic weapons after all those gun laws were passed to prevent this?" Amber Wilcox asked.

"I don't think people realize there is a black market for guns," Chandler said.

"What's a black market?" someone asked from the back of the room.

"Chandler, will you explain that for the class please?" Mr. Lopez asked.

"A black market is a place to buy goods—in this case guns— that is not a regular retail store. Like meeting someone in the parking lot to buy it."

"But why does that happen?" Brittany Andrews asked.

"Are you asking why people still buy guns, or why do people kill with them?" Mr. Lopez said.

"Both."

"Criminals don't obey laws," said Hunter Tate. "It's as simple as that."

"These are just senseless killings of innocent people," Rosa Martinez said. "Just stupid!"

"Do politicians realize that criminals won't keep the law?" Chandler asked.

"So, if gun control laws can't stop the black market, what does this country need to do?" Mr. Lopez asked.

Silence.

"How do we stop the black market?" Chandler asked.

"Is that even possible?" I said.

"Maybe we need to focus on the mental condition of people," Selena Sanchez said.

"Go on," Mr. Lopez said.

"Well, if crazy people are going to get guns anyway, maybe we find ways to identify them before they get a gun and start shooting people."

"We need to lock them up," Brittany Andrews said.

"Wait—lock them up for being crazy?" Chandler asked.

"I don't know," Brittany said. "I just want it to stop, and it seems like every month there's another shooting."

"Last month was that church shooting by that radical sackcloth in Oklahoma because he didn't believe what they believed," Chandler said. "No offense Hunter."

"It's fine," Hunter said. "The extremists are very different than my sackcloth friends."

"How do we stop people from thinking murder is the answer to their problems?" Brittany said. "That's really the issue and more gun control laws are the only answer."

More silence.

"Haven't most of these killings been revenge killings?" I asked. "It's been guys who got fired or who got bullied or the lady whose husband had an affair and left them or they thought someone or some group was doing something that would ruin their lives?"

"Not all. In some situations, that's been the cause, but others were totally random," Mr. Lopez said. "Some are not targeted at specific people. Regardless, can we just eliminate conflict?"

"That's not even possible," said a voice from the back of the room.

The more we discussed it, the more I realized there may not be a perfect solution. Gun control might help in some cases, but not all. If someone wants a gun, they can find one or even make one.

There are so many factors that cause someone to kill another human. I don't think it's possible to solve every issue. But we can try by being kind and treating everyone with respect. Even then, some crazy people could think that a knitting club for grandmas was a cover for a terrorist organization!

The news made the day very somber, and it carried over throughout the week.

Katie and I saw each other a bit during the week at school, but every night we had some other commitment. We talked on the phone a few times, especially about Monday's shooting. She felt so bad for the loss those families experienced.

I admire how caring she was toward everyone. She had a love in her heart for everyone.

Friday night was an away game against Central High School. They were not in our conference, but this was an important game for us because they were picked as one of the best teams in the state.

They were undefeated, and very good, having beat their opponents by an average of 40 points.

That was a rough game for us. Their QB was very athletic, and they had an offensive line that we could not break through. They beat us 28-7. Not a 40-point loss, but still a loss. And that hurt.

Afterwards, I kept slamming my helmet against the lockers. We expected to play better. I didn't care that they were ranked so high.

On the bus on the way home, everyone was quiet—even Chandler who usually can't stop talking.

I texted Katie. *"We lost 28-7."*

"I heard. How did you do?" she texted.

"4 tackles, 1 QB pressure but no sacks," I replied.

"What are you doing tonight?" I wrote, hoping to see her. I knew being with Katie would cheer me up.

"I'm going to a party at Susan's house. Wanna come?"

Susan Johnson lived next to Katie on their cul-de-sac. Susan, Sarah, and Kellie—all Katie's besties—lived on the same street since kindergarten. They often had parties, even when their parents were home. Susan's parents didn't care much, or perhaps they thought it was cool to let their 18-year-old daughter bring her high school friends over to drink.

I knew there would be drinking there, but I wanted to see Katie, so I texted *"Yes, that would be fun. Can I bring Chandler?"*

"Of course. The more the merrier," Katie texted.

"Great, see you in about 30 minutes."

She replied with some heart emojis.

I was a little uncomfortable going to a party at Susan Johnson's house. I heard her parties got pretty wild. I was also uncomfortable that Katie wanted to go.

"Chandler, we are going to a party at Susan Johnson's house tonight," I said to him.

"Dude, I can't. I have to study for the ACT test tomorrow," Chandler said. "Tyson and Ben are taking it with me."

"Oh yeah, I forgot that was tomorrow."

"We should have all taken it last year when you did," Chandler said.

So, I was going to be on my own at the party.

I texted my parents and told them that some friends were going to hang out for an hour or so. I couldn't tell my parents I was going to an EDM party, or they wouldn't let me go. I knew I wouldn't drink, but I wasn't sure about Katie.

After getting off the bus, I wished my friends good luck on the ACT and headed to Susan's house.

When I got to their street, there were about 20 cars in the driveway and street. It was loud—I could hear music from the street.

Susan greeted me at the door.

"Hi Jake," she said. "Katie said you'd be coming. Welcome."

"Thank you. Nice house."

"My parents are not home, but they are ok with me having a party tonight," she said, as if it mattered for me to know that.

There was a keg of beer on the kitchen table and several bottles of other types of alcohol on the counter. Everyone had a cup. There were drinking games going on, and a few couples making out on Susan's couches.

"Jake Peterson! It's about time you showed up," Katie said.

"Hey. You look gorgeous!" I said, giving her a big hug.

"Why thank you. You don't look so bad yourself. Sorry about the game," she said.

"It's ok. Just frustrating that we thought we'd play better than we did."

"Do you want a drink?" she asked.

"Katie, you know I don't drink, right?"

"Yes. I meant soda or water. There's plenty of soda in the fridge."

"Oh, thank you. I'll just take a water."

She grabbed a bottle for me.

"Thanks. What are you drinking?" I asked.

"It's just a beer, but it's pretty good," she said taking another sip.

This was going to be an interesting night for our relationship. I wasn't sure how much of a party girl Katie was. But tonight, I was going to find out.

We hung out with a bunch of kids. There were too many people for us to have a one-on-one conversation. I was more of a quiet observer, having not been to many drinking parties.

We played a card game with eight other people. It's funny how drinking can affect people's ability to think strategically and realistically. Katie and I were partners and won easily, although I could see the impact of alcohol on Katie's actions.

After a number of shots and a couple cans of beer, Katie was fully intoxicated. She became sluggish and handsy, with slurred speech.

She was rubbing my arm, which I liked. But when Miguel Montenegro came to our table to grab a handful of chips, Katie started rubbing his arm instead. Loving the attention, he rubbed her back.

"You are so sweet," Katie said to Miguel.

"You too," Miguel said, continuing her back massage.

I was amazed at the two of them. Right in front of me. It put me in an awkward position. Katie and I weren't officially boyfriend and girlfriend yet, so I couldn't really stop their affection. But I thought we were headed toward that status.

Luckily, Katie's friend Kellie Roberts was at our table, and she knew about the two of us.

"Miguel, Katie and Jake are dating," Kellie said.

"Oh," Miguel said surprisingly as he stopped rubbing her back.

"So, get your meat hooks off her!" Kellie said jokingly.

"Sorry man," Miguel said to me. "She was rubbing my arm first. I didn't know."

"No worries Miguel," I said, as he walked away.

"Where's Miguel going?" Katie asked. "I need him to massage my back some more."

"Katie, it's ok," I said. "I'll rub your back."

"Thanks Jack."

"Ah, it's Jake," I corrected her.

"I know. I was just being funny."

"Maybe I should walk you home."

"Yes, I think I need to go home now."

I thanked everyone, and got up to leave, helping Katie up. Putting my arm around her, I helped her get to the door.

"Are you taking her home?" Susan asked.

"Yes. I don't know that she could make it on her own," I said.

"Thanks for coming."

"Thank you," I said.

Katie was sluggish and needed me to keep her from falling. I had to lift her up a few times on the short walk home.

"Are your parents home?" I asked her.

"I don't remember. I think so."

"So are you going to be in trouble," I asked, worried about her.

"No. They're cool."

But I was thinking they are going to be livid with her.

I walked her to her front door and rang the doorbell. It was about 11:00 and there were lights still on.

Katie's mom came to the door.

"Mrs. Martin, Katie drank a little too much tonight," I said.

"Hi Mom," Katie slurred.

"Thanks Jake," her mom said. "I appreciate you making sure she got home ok."

"I don't know if she's been drunk before, but I don't think she planned on it. Other kids were drinking a lot more than Katie," I said, trying to back her up.

"It's happened a couple other times," she said. "But it's ok. She's 18. Hopefully, this teaches her to not go overboard in the future."

"OK. Good night," I said.

"Are you ok to drive home, Jake?"

"Yes ma'am, I don't drink."

"That's great. I'll take her from here. Drive safe."

I was blown away. Her parents were cool with it. She was three years under the legal drinking age, but because she was 18, they let her make her own decisions. If I came home drunk, even though I was 18, my parents would ground me for the rest of my life.

I couldn't stop thinking about the whole experience. First was the way Katie acted when she was drunk. The fact that she would flirt with another guy right in front of me was concerning. I realize she was drunk, but I didn't expect her to do something like that. Second was how accepting her mom was of her actions. It made me question if I really knew Katie as well as I thought.

CHAPTER 8

SIGNS

I thought about the situation all weekend. Katie was so sick Saturday that she didn't contact me until Saturday night around eight.

"I'm so sorry about last night," she texted.

"How are you feeling?" I asked.

"I've never puked so much in my life, and I've felt sick all day, but I'm finally feeling a little better."

"I'm so sorry. I was impressed that your mom wasn't mad about it."

"Yeah, she's cool about that ever since I turned 18."

"Get some rest and I'll see you Monday."

I was so confused by who she was that I spent the entire next week silently observing her. I wanted to know who the real Katie Martin was. I asked questions, put her in difficult situations, had serious talks, and more. But nothing I saw during the week gave me an indication that she was anything but sweet and kind and loyal to her relationships—like ours. I was looking for any sign, but there were none.

I came to the conclusion that her character was as good as I had seen, and that the other side of her was only caused by alcohol. That was a relief, unless she was going to develop a drinking problem.

So, I invited her to a party at my house Friday night after the game. I told Chandler, Tyson, Ben, and a few other guys to bring a girl and come for games, pizza, and ice cream.

We beat Berea Commons High School 42-10 and I had two sacks. It was a great game. Katie waited for me after the game, and I gave her a ride to my house.

I told everyone to meet us there at 9:30, so Katie and I could set up before they got there.

My parents were gracious hosts who got a lot of food ready and then disappeared.

"Hi Katie," my mom said welcoming her. "Wasn't that a great game tonight?" she said.

"Hi Mrs. Peterson. Good to see you again," Katie said.

"Mom, can't we stay up later?" asked my sister Jane.

Jane and Zack wanted to stay up to spy on our party, but 9:30 was their bedtime.

"No dear, Jake doesn't need his brother and sister at his party," mom said. "And be sure to brush your hair good tonight before you go to bed."

"Can I help you, Jane?" Katie said. "I've always wanted a little sister."

"Sure, that's cool," Jane said. And off they went.

"I really like her Jake," mom said.

"Me too. She's very kind."

I wasn't going to tell my mom about last weekend's drinking issue. At least not yet.

In a few minutes, there was a knock at the door, and all my friends came. Tyson brought Kami with him, Chandler and Ben brought two cheerleaders, Latoya Reynolds, and Kim Garcia. There were eight of us—just the right number for games.

My friends and I play this game called Signs. You need a big group of people to play it. One person goes into another room until each of us comes up with a sign or signal that is "our sign." A sign may be sitting with your arms crossed, or putting your hand on your chin, or scratching your head. Each sign is subtle—not waving arms or anything easily noticeable so you don't get busted—and it is specific to you.

Everyone picks a unique sign and remembers the signs of others. To "send" control of the game to someone, you first act out your sign and then act out theirs. They acknowledge it by giving their sign, and then sending control to someone else by doing that person's sign. Each round begins when the person comes back into the room and tries to guess who has the sign before they send it to someone else.

If you're fast and you can see two people doing the same sign— one sending and one receiving—then you know the second one who did the sign has control. If you guess them before they send it to someone else, you win, and that person becomes the guesser. If the sign is already passed to someone else, you keep guessing.

You have to be quick to catch on.

When I'm the guesser, I'll sometimes wait and watch the signs go back and forth. Guys will try to do a fake sign, but they'll always go back to their real sign because they must use that to pass the sign. When you see repetition of the same sign, you know you got them.

It's a fun game if you're fast and alert.

Katie and I had fun with it, adding extra signs that involved me touching her knee and her running her fingers through my hair.

Tyson and Kami picked up on it and kissed passionately, as if that was one of their signs.

It was a great night of laughter and fun. And no alcohol.

Katie didn't need alcohol to party. She only drank when she was at a party with her friends. Especially Susan.

In church on Sunday, we learned about the signs of the Second Coming. They include wars, rumors of wars, bloodshed, famine, disease, earthquakes and more.

The Bible says nation shall rise against nation and kingdom against kingdom. I can't think of any nation that is not fighting (at least verbally) against another nation. Many nations hate America because of our freedoms and our laws. Many nations accuse us of things we don't do. There is tension between America and Russia, North Korea, and several countries in the Middle East. There are many other countries who hate each other and threaten war or are in the midst of war right now. That's a sign of the Second Coming.

All the signs predicted in the Book of Matthew have been happening for decades, but more so in the past few years. Devastation has been frequent and consistent. The number of those disasters has been increasing.

As the list of signs was read off in church, it became apparent that every one of those signs has either already happened or was happening now.

We read St. Mark chapter 13 and learned about wars and rumors of wars, killings, and all sorts of destruction of the earth. It even said that the stars will fall out of the sky. We learned that people would betray each other—even brother against brother.

The lesson at church had me thinking all night Sunday. Since every sign that needed to happen before the Second Coming has happened, then that meant the end was near.

That was eye-opening to me. It made me wonder if I was ready for the Second Coming. Was I good enough? Had I done enough good things? It also made me wonder what the destruction would be like and if I'd survive it.

I don't worry about what will happen to me—it's all part of God's plan. But it was definitely something that was on my mind so much that I couldn't think of much else.

"What will the end of the world be like for us?" I asked my parents at dinner.

"They say it will be both great and terrible," my dad said. "Great for those who are ready, and terrible for those who are not."

"Are we ready?" I asked.

"Do you think you are?" asked me.

"In some ways I think I am, and in others, not so much."

"You better clean your room first!" Zack joked.

"Funny," I said.

"Jake, I don't think anyone feels completely ready. Just focus on those things that you think you can improve on," dad said. "But son, you're trying to do your best at everything you do. That shows God you follow him. I think you are ready," he said.

"Most definitely," mom said. "All of you are such good kids and do so many things right," she said.

"I don't want to die," Jane said.

"Don't worry Jane, you'll be ok," mom said.

"But I mean I don't want to die in an earthquake."

"He read that stars are going to fall out of the sky," said Zack. "Imagine getting hit by a falling star!"

"That's gotta hurt," I said.

"How do we run away from stars falling out of the sky?" Jane asked.

"Honey, you're worrying about something that we know little about," mom said.

"We'll be here to protect you," dad said.

"How bad will it be for those who are not ready?" I asked.

"Terrible means terrible," dad said. "I imagine it will be a surprise and very sad for those who don't follow God like they should. There will be death, destruction, and devastation to cleanse the earth before the Second Coming."

I loved having deep conversations with my parents. They treated me like an adult and were open to my opinions.

That night, I had my family make a big sign asking Katie to homecoming. We taped a couple rolls of shop paper together to make a sign that was 56 feet wide—the total width of all four walls in Katie's bedroom.

I texted Hannah that morning and asked if she could get Katie out of the house tonight and let me tape this sign all over her room so when she opened her door, the sign is all she'd see. Hannah was excited to help.

"What time do you need her out of the house?" Hannah texted.

"How's 7:00–8:00?"

"I'll make that work. And Jeff will be home to let you in her room," She texted. She followed up with *"this is so exciting!"* and a couple heart emojis.

My whole family helped me color the sign after dinner since it was so huge. Mom penciled it out and everyone got markers and colored in a few words.

The sign read: I NEED YOUR HELP ON A "LITTLE PROJECT" CALLED HOMECOMING. WILL YOU GO WITH ME?

"What's with the 'little project?'" dad asked.

I told him the story of Mr. Stevenson's biology class, that he called Katie my little project, and ever since then, everyone calls her my little project.

We got done with the sign around 6:30 and the house had the aromatic scent of magic marker! I rolled it up and got ready to go.

"You don't take the Connector Road to her house, do you?" dad asked.

"I haven't," I said. "But isn't it ok during the day? I thought nighttime was the worst time to drive on it."

"Nighttime is terrible to be on that road, but even during the day it's bad," dad said. So many drivers have slid off that gravel road into the ditch during the day. And at night you have that danger plus the deer running across the road."

"Yeah, I don't plan on taking the Connector unless I need to."

"Please don't," mom said.

"It's worth the extra 10 minutes to be safe," dad said.

"That's what Katie told me."

"Well listen to your girlfriend," dad said.

I headed over to Katie's, so I'd be there around 7:10, giving Hannah and Katie a 10-minute cushion.

Jeff answered the door.

"Come on in Jake," he said. "I'll take you to Katie's room."

"Thanks Jeff," I said, still getting used to calling him by his first name.

"Do you need any help?"

"Ah, yes, you could help hold up the sign while I tape it to the wall," I said. "I brought blue painter's tape, so it wouldn't leave a mark."

"Smart man. Thank you for that," he said.

Katie's room was immaculate. She was a tidy person, but I didn't realize she could actually be a clean freak!

"What's the plan?" Jeff asked.

"If you roll out a little bit of the sign at a time, I'll follow you and tape it down."

"OK," he said as he stood in one corner holding the sign and I stood on a chair ready to tape the sign by her door.

That made it go easy. I taped as he unrolled it all around the room. I couldn't have done it without him.

And when we were done, the sign stretched from the right side of her door, across all four walls and ended by the left side of the door.

Thanks to Hannah for giving me an exact measurement!

It looked great.

I thanked Jeff and headed home.

I think life is all about signs. Everything is a sign. The way you act is a sign of what you believe. The way you dress is a sign of what you think about yourself. Signs on the road tell us where to go or not go, which direction and how fast. What you talk about is a sign of what's important to you. If you decide to help people or not help them, that's a sign that says a lot about your character. If you spend more time on your phone than talking to your date, that's a sign to your date that she's not that important. And devastating events are signs that the Second Coming is happening soon.

The next day at football practice, I got my answer from Katie. We were doing drills practicing intercepting the football. While every other defender didn't intercept the ball, when it was my turn, coach threw the ball right at me.

"You're making it too easy on me coach," I laughed.

I threw the ball back to him and he threw it right back.

"What's up coach?"

"Check out that ball."

Katie had bought a football and painted on it: "I'm in! Let's have a ball at Homecoming, Love Katie."

That was quite some effort to arrange that. I was impressed.

Of course, Chandler had to give me crap about it.

"You're wasting valuable practice time to deal with some homecoming issues?"

"Dude, you're just jealous."

CHAPTER 9

HOMECOMING

Three weeks later was Homecoming. It was always a fun week at school with assemblies, hall decorating, a parade, the game, and the dance.

Katie and I had become very close during those three weeks. She hadn't gone to any EDM drinking parties because I kept asking her out every Friday and Saturday night, so she didn't have any time to go. One night we'd do something fun like dinner and a concert or something. The other night we'd hang at her house or mine. My family loved her. Jane especially connected with her, and she loved when Katie would join our family for games or a movie. Katie was the sister Jane never had.

Katie was always asking me questions when we were alone—even after three weeks. I don't know where all her questions came from. But at this point I felt like she knew everything about me, and I knew everything about her. And I love her. I really do. But I wasn't ready to tell her that yet.

We only saw each other between two classes each day, and we were going opposite directions both times. But we didn't let that passing happen without a hug and kiss.

Homecoming game was going to be fun. It was against Presser Tech, a team that was 1-6 on the year. We should beat them easily. We were 5-3 with all our losses to highly ranked teams.

That Friday morning every student was given a card to vote for the king and queen of Homecoming. Couples submitted their names for the voting last week. I didn't really care to be involved with that, but Katie submitted our names and so did a few of our friends.

There were 10 couples on the voting card. In addition to me and Katie, Tyson and Kami were on the list. They were still a couple—probably because they were the best in the entire school at making out in the halls.

The results of the voting would be announced at halftime of the game, and the winners would be crowned king and queen of the Homecoming dance, complete with a crown and cape. So, everyone running for king and queen were supposed to wear their dresses and suits to the football game, unless they were on the team.

The assembly during last hour of the day was a lot like the first one of the year. Cheers, introduction of the team, and the band playing our fight song. We were pumped. Everyone wants to win their Homecoming game.

The game went as expected. We were up 28-0 at half time, and both Chandler and I each had a sack. Instead of going into the locker room at halftime, the guys who were running for Homecoming king went to an area behind the bleachers where we met our dates.

Katie was dressed in a light pink dress with gorgeous hair and makeup. She really was the prettiest girl in the school. And I was lucky to have her as my girlfriend.

"Wow. You look absolutely stunning!" I said.

"Why thank you, Jake Peterson," she said.

"Jake Peterson and Katie Martin, please come over here" said a teacher on a megaphone.

"You two will be riding in this convertible" she said, pointing to a red convertible. "You'll both sit on the back of the car with your feet on the back seat," she said. "Don't worry, the car won't go more than five miles per hour."

Everyone running for Homecoming royalty was going to sit in a convertible that would ride along the track between the football field and the bleachers. The cars stopped at the 50-yard line where each couple would get out and the guy would take his date by the arm and walk to the center of the field until all couples got there. Then, someone would announce the winners of the voting.

We were the fourth car in the parade. We felt like royalty as we rode along the track. As we approached the 50-yard line, the announcer said, "Katie Martin and Jake Peterson." The crowd cheered for us. I went around the car and opened her door for her. The crowd cheered at that even more.

"Why thank you, your Highness," Katie said.

"Anything for my little project," I said.

She laughed. She looked gorgeous, but she was wearing high heels that were digging into the grass, making it hard for her to walk. So, I put my arm around her and lifted her gently as she walked.

We stood on a red carpet in the center of the field with the other royalty and waited until the others got there.

When the last couple got to the center, the announcer said, "Now it's time to reveal the results of voting for the West View High School Homecoming King and Queen."

The audience cheered loudly.

"We will announce the second runner up, then the first runner-up and then your King and Queen. The second runner-up is... Kami Donahoe and Tyson Jensen."

"My man Tyson!" I yelled. "Congrats."

Everyone clapped and cheered. Kami took the opportunity to kiss Tyson again.

"The first runner-up is.... Latisha Jones and Tommy Swenson."

They were a cool couple and well deserved.

"Do you think it's us?" Katie said.

"And now...," said the announcer.

"I don't think so," I said. "There are too many great couples here."

"This year's Homecoming King and Queen are..."

The announcer played a drumroll recording to add suspense.

"Jake Peterson and Katie Martin!"

"We won!" Katie said.

"Wow, I'm shocked," I said hugging her.

Ms. Parker, my student council director, brought us both crowns and gave me a red cape and Katie a white shawl.

"Congratulations" Ms. Parker said. "Well deserved!"

"Jake, we did it!" Katie said.

I was shocked. The crowd was excited for us. And we posed for pictures from the yearbook committee and the local newspaper.

We felt like royalty. Everyone congratulated us.

We walked back to our convertible and got in for a ride back to the area behind the bleachers where we started.

"Jake, get me one more sack tonight," she said.

"You got it, my queen," I promised. I kissed her, ran to the sidelines, and grabbed my helmet to get ready for the second half.

The second half was more of what happened in the first half. Both Chandler and I got a sack in the second half and then coach pulled us.

"What a game you played," I said to Chandler, as we walked off the field.

"I'm just trying to be like the king," he said.

"Dude, I'm shocked that we won Homecoming King and Queen," I said.

"It was all because of Katie. They didn't pick you two because of you," he joked.

We went over to the sideline, and Chandler grabbed my crown and cape and put them on. He ran up and down the sidelines and the crowd went wild.

Coach let a lot of underclassmen and subs play. That was a good thing. Some coaches don't ever take out their starters unless there's an injury. But our subs needed time to play in a real game to get experience and gain confidence.

Chandler and I cheered them on from our sidelines. We were yelling and cheering at them all and that motivated them to do well. They knew we were there to support them. It was a great feeling to see the younger guys play well.

We won 42-7. Every one of our guys played a great game, and we were now 6-3.

Katie had changed and came down to the field. She ran up to me and jumped in my arms. "Great game my king!" she said.

"Where's your dress?"

"I needed to get comfortable for the rest of the night."

"Does my little project have big plans for us tonight?"

"Oh yeah."

"Well, I better go shower and try to smell a little better then."

"Yes, please," she joked.

"Wait for me outside the locker room, and I'll hurry," I said with a kiss.

Chandler ran over to me. "Come on, man, coach wants to do a quick game recap."

We hustled into the locker room, and everyone was pumped. When the subs play well, everyone is excited.

"Guys, great game tonight," coach said. "When everyone does their assignments exactly and stays focused, this is what happens."

"It helped that Presser sucks!" said a player in the back, which resulted in a lot of laughs.

Coach Davidson laughed. "Then it's a good thing we won big, or you'd all be in big trouble!"

Players laughed.

"Now get showered and go enjoy Homecoming weekend," coach said.

I showered and got ready fast. Katie and I had a date tonight. Just us. None of her girlfriends. None of my buddies. Just the two of us.

When I walked out, Katie was standing by the fence talking to two guys with Presser Tech jackets on. She looked scared.

"Jake!" she called out to me in a scared voice.

I ran over to her. "What's going on guys?" I asked.

They were two bigger guys who I didn't recognize from the game. I think the Presser player's bus left already. They looked older and may have even graduated a few years ago.

"Is this your girlfriend?" one of them asked.

"Yes, it is," I said as I moved between her and the two guys. I grabbed Katie and walked away from them backwards, keeping an eye on them.

"Where are you going? We just want to talk with her a bit," they said following me.

"Guys, I think you are scaring her. That's not cool."

"Are you calling us scary?" one of them said.

Just then some of the other players walked out of the locker room. These Presser guys may have thought I was the last West View player. Or maybe they just didn't think.

Ben and Tyson could sense something was wrong and came running over.

"Need some help, Jake?" Ben said.

"That'd be great."

"You want to fight us?" one of the Presser guys said.

"No. I want you to go home and stop bothering girls," I said.

"Or what?" he responded, puffing out his chest.

Just then Chandler and a couple other guys came out. Tyson motioned them to come over. Now it was seven on two.

"Do you really think you're going to beat seven of us?" I said.

"Come on guys. It's not worth it. No one wants to get hurt tonight," I said.

My teammates stood in a line looking at the two Presser guys, who weren't moving.

"Guys, let's all just go home," Chandler added.

The bigger Presser guy said "let's go" to his friend. They walked away without saying anything more.

We all watched to make sure they had didn't turn around and come back.

"That was smart of them to walk away," Chandler said.

"Even if they got in a few good hits, we would have overpowered them," said Ben.

"Thank you, guys," Katie said, still shaking.

"Yes, thank you," I said.

"It's all good," Chandler said. "We'll see you guys tomorrow."

"Try not to get in any more fights tonight," Tyson said.

"Tell that to Katie, she started it," Ben said.

I hugged Katie tight. "I'm so sorry that happened to you," I said.

"Jake, I was so scared. Thank you for protecting me," she said.

We stood there on the field for a minute holding each other. Then I grabbed her hand and said, "Let's get out of here."

When we got to my car, she was still a mess.

"Jake, what if you didn't come out of the locker room for five more minutes? What would have happened to me?"

"I'm glad I came out when I did."

"I can't thank you enough. That was frightening."

"What if we just go to your house tonight and relax," I said. "I think that would help you."

"I think that's a good idea. I'm so glad you're flexible."

"Of course. It's more important that you feel safe than anything else."

"Oh Jake Peterson, you are so cool!" she said, kissing my cheek.

She texted her parents to tell them we were coming to her house. She told them about the incident with the guys. When we got to her house, her parents wanted to hear the whole story.

"It was awful," she said. "They started out acting nice, and then they got weird fast."

"Like what?" Jeff said.

"One of them grabbed my arm and said I needed to go out with him tonight," Katie said.

"And then they said rude things they wanted to do with me," she said.

"Oh my gosh," said Hannah.

"What happened next?" Jeff asked.

"That's when I saw Jake coming out of the locker room and I called over to him. He saved me."

"Jake, we are so glad you came out of the locker room when you did," Hannah said as she hugged Katie.

"Yes, thank you Jake," Jeff said.

"Luckily, other players came out right behind me. Those guys didn't want a seven on two fight," I said.

"He's being too humble," Katie said. "He stood right between me and those two guys and was ready to fight them both."

"I think we all need some ice cream," said Hannah. "Doesn't that sound good right now?"

"Yes," Katie said.

We all talked as we ate ice cream. Chocolate peanut butter for me and Katie. Chocolate chip mint for Hannah and Rocky Road for Jeff.

As we talked, I felt a connection with Jeff and Hannah. They cared so much for Katie. And they are just cool. Both are like older siblings more than the parents of my girlfriend.

I also think they respected me and appreciated that I was so respectful of their daughter. I can't imagine what a father feels about the guys who date his daughter. I don't think it will be easy for me either. But if the guy has a personality, and isn't all over my daughter, I will know she's in good hands.

Katie had settled down by the time we were done with our ice cream.

"Hey, we should all play cards," Hannah said.

"Yeah, let's do it," Katie said. "Dad and Jake, what do you think?"

"You bet," Jeff said.

"Sure," I said. "But first, I have a present for you."

"You do?" Katie said.

"Yes. You shuffle the cards and I need to get something from my car."

"What is it?" Katie asked.

"Hold on, I'll go get it," I said.

I ran out to my car and grabbed an envelope that I'd had been hiding in my glove box for a week.

I ran back into the house with the envelope. I just opened the door and walked in. It felt like home. The three of them were sitting around the table with cards already delt.

"What is it, Jake?" Katie asked again.

"Well, it's a special present for you that I hope you'll love forever," I said, handing her the envelope.

"It looks like an envelope full of cash," Jeff joked.

"Open it," Hannah said.

Katie opened it and busted up laughing. "I love it!" she said. She turned the paper around to her parents and revealed a bumper sticker for her Hummer. It was pink with big black letters "Jake's Little Project."

"That's so funny," Hannah said. "Where did you ever get that?"

"I ordered it online."

"I want to put it on my Hummer right now," Katie said.

Jeff grabbed a couple of paper towels, and we all headed out to the driveway. He cleaned off the front right bumper and dried it for Katie.

"This is going to be right here on my front bumper so everyone will see it and know that I am your little project," Katie said.

"Wait until Mr. Stevenson sees it," I joked.

We all laughed.

When Katie put it on her Hummer, it seemed to cement our relationship right there. It had a feeling of commitment to it.

I had a great night with her and her family. The laughter continued all night, as we played cards and joked. It was great to be with her parents and get to know them better. And most importantly, I was glad Katie was safe.

The next day when Katie went to get her hair done, every stylist at her salon asked about the pink bumper sticker. She loved telling everyone the story behind it.

We didn't see each other all day. But at 4:30, it was time to get ready. I was excited for the night ahead. I got dressed in the tux I rented, grabbed the king's crown and cape, and Katie's corsage.

My car was at the shop for the weekend, so I got to drive my parent's car tonight. I was picking up Chandler first and then we were picking up the girls.

While I was in a traditional black tuxedo, white shirt and black bow tie, Chandler was in a black tux coat but lime green pants and a flowered bow tie.

"Dude, what's with those pants?" I asked him when he got in the car.

"Don't you just love them man?" Chandler said. "They're so rad!"

We first went to get Chandler's date —Tara Innsbrook. She was a free spirit that fit Chandler's personality very well. Chandler is an "anything goes" kind of guy. Not irresponsible, but just without worries about much of anything.

Tara was the female version of Chandler—funny and could be the life of any party. I don't think she was an EDM, but it wouldn't surprise me if she was.

Tara wore a lime green dress with feathers on it that matched Chandler's pants.

"You look great Tara!" I said.

"Thanks Jake. You look like you're running for president," she said.

"I already am," I said.

They both laughed.

We drove to Katie's house next. Tyson and Ben and their dates were going to meet us there in a few minutes and we were all going to have pictures taken in Katie's back yard. Then the eight of us were going to dinner and then the dance.

We parked at Katie's house and went up to the door. I opened it and walked in, which surprised Chandler and Tara.

"Dude, are they ok with you just walking in?" Chandler asked.

"Yes."

"Jake, you look so handsome," Hannah said, giving me a big hug.

"I guess they're ok with it," Chandler said quietly to Tara.

"Katie, Jake's here!" Hannah yelled up the stairs.

"Hannah, this is my best friend Chandler and his date Tara," I said.

"Those are very colorful and creative outfits," Hannah said politely.

Just then, Katie appeared at the top of the stairs. My heart was pounding fast. She really took my breath away as she walked down the stairs.

"Wow!" I said, giving her a big hug.

"All right guys, enough with the mushy stuff," Chandler said. "We need to take pictures so I can eat. I'm starving."

The doorbell rang and it was Ben, Tyson, and their dates. But I didn't even hear it. I was in a zone hugging Katie.

"Let's go guys. Time for pictures!"

We all walked through Katie's house to their back yard—the eight of us and about 14 parents who came to take photos and send us off. Both my parents came, and I introduced them to Jeff and Hannah.

"We love Katie," my mom said to Jeff and Hannah. "She is the sweetest girl and so polite and kind."

"Well, your Jake has to be the most mature senior I've ever met," Hannah said.

"Yes, a true gentleman," Jeff said.

"Don't they look great together?" Hannah said.

Sometimes pictures are more important to parents than the students. So, we patiently waited through it.

After a half hour or so later, we were finally done with pictures and needed to go. We said goodbye to the parents and went on our way.

Dinner was so fun with everyone. These guys have been my friends and been by my side through four years of high school. I was taking in every moment, realizing this was the last time we'd be together for a homecoming event.

The dance was a blast. As senior class president, I helped pick the band and decided on decorations and refreshments. But tonight, I got to enjoy it all without doing any of the set up or clean up.

The eight of us danced together a lot and were crazy a lot. That brought lots of laughter throughout the night.

Katie and I couldn't wait for the slow songs. Not that we didn't want to be with everyone else, but that we wanted a little alone time.

"I'm having such a great night," Katie said holding me close during a slow song.

"Me too," I said. "And I'm so lucky to be your date."

"I'm so lucky to be your little project!" she joked.

We held each other close as we danced.

"I am so in love with you," I said.

I wasn't sure how she'd take that. But I didn't care. I needed her to know.

"Oh Jake, I love you too," she said. "I've felt this way for a while but didn't want to scare you off by telling you too soon."

When we kissed on the dance floor, everything and everyone else seemed to fade away. I don't know if I'd ever been happier in my life.

The rest of the night was magical. My heart was full, and she was so incredible. I felt like she was a huge blessing in my life.

After the dance, we all went out to Nielsons for ice cream.

Katie and I had fun with Chandler and Tara on the way. We got along great. At Nielsons with Tyson and Kami, and Ben and Olivia, all eight of us had a blast together.

We weren't the only kids at Nielsons from our Homecoming dance. A bunch of EDM's were there, some already wasted from whatever they'd been smoking or drinking at the dance. Some of them couldn't even sit up straight they were so wasted. I don't think ice cream was going to make them sober.

"It's so sad," Tara said.

"What?" Katie asked.

"That they get so wasted every chance they get," Tara said.

"My parents would kill me if I got wasted even once," Olivia said.

Everyone laughed.

"What do you guys think?" Tara asked.

"Yeah, it's crazy," I said. "Not sure how they are going to function with a job and family if they are already addicted to things before they get out of high school."

"You don't mean that no one should ever drink alcohol, do you?" Katie asked.

"I'm not saying that," I said.

"Because not everyone has made the same commitment that you have," Katie said.

"I understand. I realize adults drink and that's their decision," I said. "But my concern is if these kids are already addicted before they become adults, that could be a problem."

"I agree," Chandler piped in. "I'm not opposed to drinking when I'm old enough, but you've got to have some maturity to it."

"That's probably why the legal drinking age is 21 and not 16," Ben said.

"Jake, you aren't going to drink?" Olivia asked. "Why?"

"My grandparents died in a car accident caused by a drunk driver. That kind of scared me into the decision not to drink."

"Jake's a guy that basically never breaks the rules," Chandler said.

"Dude—he doesn't even bend the rules!" Tyson said.

Everyone laughed.

"I still love him," Katie said as she grabbed my arm.

We looked at Tyson and Kami, who were all over each other. They had spent more time making out at the dance than dancing.

"An even bigger problem than teenage drinking is Tyson and Kami always swapping spit!" Chandler said.

Everyone laughed. Tyson held up a finger mid-kiss, as if to say, "give me a minute." That made everyone laugh more.

Then we realized it was midnight, and Nielson's was closing.

"Should we get going?" Tyson said. "I need to get her home."

"You two might need a chaperone tonight," Chandler said.

Everyone laughed again.

As we all got up, I pulled Tyson aside for a minute. I was worried about where his relationship was going.

"Tyson, be careful tonight," I said to him privately.

"What do you mean?" he asked.

"Just don't do anything with Kami that you might regret later. Be sure."

"I'm fine. Don't worry about us man."

I said my peace but was still worried about the two of them. Sometimes it's hard to deal with the fact that people have freedom to make their own decisions.

"What did you say to Tyson?" Katie asked.

"I just told him to be careful tonight. I worry about where the two of them might end up tonight."

"You are always so thoughtful."

"He's a great friend, and I'd hate to see him mess up his future."

As we drove home, we were all a bit quiet, soaking up the excitement and fun of the night. I couldn't stop thinking about how perfect tonight was for Katie and me. She and I were so good for each other. I had never felt this way about anyone before.

CHAPTER 10

KATIE IS HOT!

T hree months later, Katie and I were even more serious. It was late-January and even though the weather was cold, Katie was hot!

Katie was so hot that when she walked into a room, the AC automatically turned on.

She was so hot, she was banned from flying to the polar ice caps.

Katie was so hot, she single-handedly made global warming a bigger problem than it already was.

She was so hot that when she opened a freezer, it instantly defrosted.

When she jumped in a pool, the water instantly got hot.

We had developed a bond so strong that I don't think it could be broken. We had become so comfortable with each other and our families, that at times, it even felt like we were married.

Katie was great. The only issue I had was that she was still occasionally drinking with the Eat, Drink & Be Merry group. She only went to a few parties, but they were not a great place for her to be—at least in my opinion.

We went to a couple parties together last fall and at first, she wouldn't drink to be respectful of me. But at a couple parties during Christmas, she decided to "have just a little." With her small frame and young age, just a few drinks got her drunk.

When she wasn't around alcohol, she was so great – charming, intelligent, personable, and fun. But at these parties, when she had a couple drinks, she became a different person – loud, sloppy, flirty with other guys, and sometimes even rude.

We had talked about it after a few Christmas parties. But I had to be careful not to push my beliefs on her, knowing that she did not make the same promise about drinking that I had made. I was conflicted. I had hoped that she would decide not to drink, but I couldn't ask her to change her life for me. I was just trying to deal with how different she was when she drank.

The whole month of January and into early February, I kept going out with her every Friday and Saturday, so she wouldn't be free for many parties. That only worked for so long, and then Katie told me her friends were complaining that they didn't see her on weekends anymore.

That Sunday afternoon, Katie came over for dinner like she had every Sunday for the past couple months. It was a time where Katie and my family got to know each other better. She and Jane had become great friends. I loved that.

After dinner, Katie and I were on the couch cuddling up.

"I have something for you," she said, pulling out an envelope from her purse.

"Wow, you never stop surprising me," I said.

"Open it," she said.

It was a card inviting me to a Valentines dinner—her treat—followed by a party at Susan's house.

"That sounds great," I said.

"Dinner is a surprise, but you're going to love it. Are you ok with the party? I know you don't like the drinking parties, but we don't need to stay long. I just haven't done anything with Susan and the girls for a long time and I want you to love my friends as much as I love yours."

"Yes, that's fine," I said. "As long as we're together on Valentine's Day, I'm happy."

"Thanks Jake. I love you."

"I love you too."

On Valentine's Day, she came to pick me up in her Hummer—which still had the pink bumper sticker "Jake's Little Project" on the front bumper.

She was so excited to take the lead on our date. It was so cute to have her come to the door to pick *me* up.

I jokingly took a little extra time to get ready, since she often did that to me. I was ready but let her sit in my living room for a minute as I overheard their discussion.

"Where are you guys going tonight?" my mom asked.

"We're going out to a fancy steak dinner and then to a party," Katie said.

"You didn't take the Connector Road to get over here, did you?" mom asked.

"No, my parents don't want me to drive on it since I hit a deer there last year. It totaled my car."

"I'm so sorry Katie. Jake told me about that and said that's why they got you the Hummer."

"Yes. They figured that I would be safer, but I haven't even taken it on the Connector ever."

"That's good. It's not worth driving on that road," mom said.

That's when I came out. "Hi Katie. Sorry I'm late, I couldn't get my hair to look good," I joked.

"Ha. You look great."

"You too. Thanks for keeping her company mom, I said.

"Always happy to visit with our Katie," mom said. "You two have fun tonight."

"Thanks Mrs. Peterson. We should be home before midnight—I know that's Jake's curfew."

We walked out the door holding hands. Since she was taking control of the whole night, she even opened my door for me. That felt a little weird, but I went with it. It felt weirder to me that she opened her car door by herself.

"When are you going to tell me where we're going for dinner?" I said.

"Why Jake Peterson, you are itching to know, aren't you? You can't handle the fact that I made some plans and you have absolutely no idea what's going on, huh?"

"HA. I'm totally fine with you being in control. Can you at least tell me what kind of food we're having?"

"You are getting the best steak dinner in town," Katie said.

"Wow. You mean The Gilroy?"

The Gilroy was a swanky steak restaurant that was expensive but had the reputation for being the best. You could easily spend $200-$300 on a dinner for two.

"Jake Peterson, you are so smart," she said, letting me know I guessed it.

"And you are so cool in every way."

"Thank you."

Dinner was every bit as good as we were told it would be. And Katie spent $267 with tip.

"Thank you so much for dinner. It was so good," I said.

"It was really good, huh?! The steak was the best I've even had. And even that bacon mac & cheese was to die for!" she said.

"Oh my gosh, yes!"

"Now are you ready for the party?"

"Let's go," I said, on board with anything after that meal.

We drove to Katie's house, parked her Hummer there and walked over to Susan's house.

Susan's house was rockin. There were 40 or more kids there and once again, Susan's parents were not home for the weekend, but left her in charge of the liquor cabinet.

"Hey guys! Happy Valentine's Day! So glad to see you," Susan said with a drink in her hand.

"Katie!" Kellie said. "Hi Jake."

"Hi Kellie. You look especially nice tonight," I said.

"Such a gentleman," Kellie said.

"Come on," Katie said grabbing my hand. "Let's go play a game with everyone."

"What are you guys drinking?" Susan asked.

"A beer," Katie said.

"Water for me," I said.

"Come on Jake, no alcohol tonight?" Susan asked. "Jake, you have to lighten up and break the rules sometime."

Everyone laughed.

Sarah asked, "Have you ever had a beer?"

"Guys, back off," Katie said. "His grandparents were killed by a drunk driver, and he made a commitment not to drink in honor of them."

Everyone seemed good with that answer.

"That's cool," Susan said.

"Let's play the 'Never Have I Ever' game. Each person says something they have not done. If anyone in the group has done that thing, those people have to take a big swig of their drink. If your drink is empty, you get another one. Everyone got that," Susan asked.

All good. She sat 12 of us in a circle around their kitchen table. And she started the game.

"I'll go first," Susan said.

"Never have I ever been to church," she said.

"Really?" a few people asked as everyone else took a swig.

"Never have I ever had sex," said Miguel Montenegro, one of Susan's friends.

"Wow—you're hitting the serious topics right away!" said Kellie, as she took a drink.

Five other people took drinks too. The group joked with them and asked for details. But only Kellie shared.

"It was junior year after prom. We were both a little wasted, but it was so romantic..."

"All right, enough of that!" Sarah joked. "We don't want the details!"

"It's your turn Ricky," Sarah said loudly to shut Kellie up.

Ricky Delfino was an EDM poster boy. He looked the part with long shaggy hair and clothes that never knew an iron. Kind of looked like a surfer dude. He was laid back and funny. Popular and a partier.

"Never have I ever sent naked pictures of myself to anyone," Ricky said.

"Oh man!" Kellie said as she took another drink. Susan and Sarah both took a drink too.

The three girls were the only ones to take a drink. I was beginning to learn a lot about Katie's friends and realized that she was the rule keeper in the group. Maybe that's why I loved her.

"You girls rock," Miguel said. "I love you all!"

"OK, it's Sarah's turn," Susan said.

"Never have I ever stolen something," Sarah said.

Then Katie took a drink!

"Katie?" I said in shock. "You stole something?"

"Oh no, there's trouble in paradise," Sarah said to the laughter of others.

"Do share," Kellie said.

"When I was little, like six years old, I was with my mom in a store where they had bulk candy," Katie said. "And I saw a candy I liked so I took it and opened the wrapper and ate it before my mom saw."

"Did you get busted?" Susan asked.

"My mom saw the candy in my mouth and asked what I had done. When I told her, she told me I was stealing and made me promise to never do that again. I had to apologize to the store owner. It was tragic."

"Jake, are you going to break up with her now that you know she's a criminal?" Kellie joked.

"No, it's cool," I said. "She was young."

"Jake, you are the best at this game because you haven't done anything wrong in your entire life," Kellie said.

"Perhaps," I joked along. "I'm realizing my only drink was for going to church, and I'm getting thirsty. Susan, I need clarification on the rules—I need a drink. Can I just take a drink of my water even though I haven't done any of these things?"

"No Jake, no drink until you have done the thing someone says they haven't done," Susan said. "Do you ever break any rules?"

Everyone laughed.

Katie was next. "Never have I ever played on a football team," she said, sensing my need to quench my thirst.

"Thank you!" I shouted and took a big swig of water.

Everyone laughed.

"My turn," I said. "Never have I ever... had an older sibling."

About half the group had to take a drink.

Spencer Marshall was next. "Never have I ever been friends with a sackcloth."

There were some laughs and some people who said Spencer was rude. But Katie and I were the only ones to take a drink. I've made friends with the sackcloths because you can never have too many friends. Plus, I wanted sackcloths to know that everyone could be their friends.

The game went on for about an hour. Katie drank a lot when the "never-have-I-evers" got more generic, like "never have I ever" been a girl, had hair below my shoulders, worn a toe ring, and got my ears pierced. Susan said "never have I ever got in a wreck on the Connector" to make sure Katie took another drink.

Three others had been in a wreck on the Connector.

I could tell Katie was more than just buzzed, and that was the point where I felt like I should take her home.

"You ready to go home?" I asked.

"No, I'm having too much fun," Katie said.

"OK, we'll stay a little longer. I'm just worried you are a little drunk," I said quietly.

"I'm not drunk," she said sluggishly and loud.

"Yes, you are," Sarah said with a laugh.

"Why do you wanna take me home?" Katie asked seductively.

"You've had enough to drink," I said, trying to be kind.

"You want to sleep with me tonight, don't you?"

"What?" I said surprised by her question. "No. Not like this."

"You don't? Why won't you sleep with me?"

"Let's talk about it at your house," I said quietly.

"Jake doesn't want to sleep with me. Am I not pretty enough?" she said.

"Katie, let's go," I said.

"If you won't sleep with me, maybe Miguel or Ricky will. Ricky, will you sleep with me tonight?"

All the girls laughed at her question.

Ricky looked at me. He knew the right answer. "No Katie, you're Jake's girlfriend."

"Come on Katie, let me take you home," I said.

"Then we can sleep together?" she asked.

"Go for it Katie!" Sarah shouted.

"He won't do it," Susan said. "He's not a rule breaker."

I was done. I felt I was patient long enough. I tried my best to be a team player during the party. But I didn't like where this party was going. A buzzed or drunk Katie was not the same Katie who I loved.

We stood up to leave, with me holding Katie's arm.

As we took a few steps, she said "Jake, I feel like I'm going to..."

Then she vomited all over the kitchen floor. And then puked again all over me and her.

I sat her down while I grabbed paper towels and cleaned it up. Sarah and Susan came over to help me.

"Katie's so funny," Susan said.

"Yeah, funny," I said, wondering how they found humor in what happened tonight.

Then, I picked Katie up and headed for the door.

"Thanks for coming guys," Susan said.

"See you guys," everyone said as we left.

I held Katie up by her waist and walked her out the door and over to her house.

"I'm sorry Jake," Katie said as we walked.

"It's ok, let's just get you home," I said.

We walked up to her house. The door was unlocked so we walked in and I helped her in and laid her on the couch in her living room. I didn't want to take her to her bedroom in fear her parents would think I had bad intentions.

I laid her down and got a blanket for her. She was asleep within a minute. I stroked her hair for a minute, told her I loved her, and kissed her forehead.

I locked the front door behind me and walked out of her house, still disturbed by Katie's actions when she was drunk. Then I realized since Katie picked me up tonight, I didn't have a way home. So, I walked back to Susan's house.

I saw Ricky walking out.

"Hey Ricky, can you give me a ride home tonight?" I asked.

"Sure."

Ricky was a funny kid. I liked him even if I didn't agree with his EDM party lifestyle.

"That was so fun tonight," he said. "Are you going to come to more parties?"

"I'm not sure. Kind of depends on Katie."

"You really have never drank even a beer?"

"No. Not one."

"That's a cool way to honor your grandparents," Ricky said.

"Thanks."

"And it's cool that you are ok with Katie drinking, even though you don't."

"Has she always been that way when she gets drunk?"

"Yeah. She's a funny drunk. Some girls are quiet drunks, but Katie is hilarious."

"Hilarious," I repeated.

"It bothers you?"

"Wouldn't it bother you if your girlfriend was asking guys to sleep with her?"

"Good point. But I don't think she meant it."

"I agree, but what if the guy she asks doesn't know that?"

"Another good point," Ricky said, as we pulled up to my house.

"Thanks for the ride, Ricky. I'll see you Monday."

"See you man. Thanks for hanging out with us tonight."

CHAPTER 11

AGONY

I was conflicted. I was in love with Katie, but I was only in love with the sober Katie, not the EDM Katie.

I couldn't sleep that night. I had been to two parties with her recently and at both of them, she flirted with other guys right in front of me. What if I wasn't there? Some guy would definitely take advantage of her if she asked him to sleep with her.

How do I deal with her desire to hang with the EDM party crowd and still love her the same? I didn't know what to do. I would never think about breaking up with her, but I didn't know if we could stay together if she was going to keep acting the way she did when she was drunk. And I was not going to tell her she had to stop drinking because of me. She has to be herself and I have to be me. But for the first time since I met her, I wondered if we could be happy together.

It was all I could think about. Even the next day after church, it was still consuming my thoughts.

"Is Katie coming over for dinner today?" mom asked.

Katie had an open invitation to come every Sunday for dinner and games, and she came over most Sundays.

"I'm not sure. I have not talked with her yet today," I said.

"Everything ok?" Mom asked perceptively.

"Ah, I'm not sure," I said.

"What's going on?"

"Well, she has gone to some drinking parties."

"Oh," mom said.

"And I've gone to a few with her to make sure she's ok and get her home safe." Before my mom could ask, I said "but I don't drink. I've kept the commitment I made to never drink."

"Oh good. Are you upset that she drinks? You know you can't set rules for her life, right?"

"I know. I'm struggling with the fact that she's drinking and I'm wondering why I'm just about the only one who doesn't drink. But also, I don't like the drunk Katie. She flirts with other guys when she's drinking."

"Oh, that's not good. She flirts with other guys while you're right there with her?"

"Yep."

"If you weren't there and she sends a guy the wrong message, that could be a big problem."

"Yeah, I know. That's what worries me. I really care about her and would hate to know some guy took advantage of her when she really didn't want that."

"So, what are you going to do?" mom asked.

"I don't know. It's been bothering me since I got home last night."

"Well, if you want my opinion, I'd suggest a couple things."

"What?"

"First, you need to talk to Katie and tell her how you feel. Great relationships are great because both parties communicate."

"Yeah, I get that."

"Second, you should give it time. Some things work themselves out with time. You need to be you and let her be her and see how that goes."

"OK."

"And finally, I would suggest you pray about it. Ask God to give you some direction for this situation and He will."

"Thanks Mom," I said, giving her a hug.

I texted Katie and asked if she was coming over for dinner.

"*Yes, if you'll have me,*" she texted back. She knew I was frustrated.

"*Definitely. See you at six,*" I responded.

She came over and was looking so gorgeous as always. My sober Katie was back, and she was her wonderful self!

"I love you," she said, hugging me at the door.

"Love you too," I said.

"Katie!" said Jane. "Come help me with my math homework."

"Is that ok, Jake?" Katie asked since we only saw each other for about a minute.

"Definitely, go help her," I said.

I went into the kitchen to help mom. "How can I help?"

"If you'd put water in the glasses and put them on the table, that would be a big help."

"Sure," I said.

"Are you going to talk with her tonight?"

"I'm planning on it, if I can get some time alone."

"Why don't you go on a walk after dinner? That would be a good way to be alone to talk it out."

I loved my mom so much. She was wise, helpful and one of my biggest fans. Some kids go through high school hating their parents, but I loved both of mine so much. They made me the man I am, and I wouldn't be as happy or successful as I was without them.

"Can you get Jane and Katie?" mom asked. "We're ready to eat."

I went into Jane's room and heard them laughing and talking. I waited at the door for a minute, just listening. Jane and Katie had a bond that would last forever, even if Katie and I ever broke up.

"We're ready to eat," I said.

"Great, I'm starving," Katie said, grabbing my hand. "You hungry Jane?"

"Yep, let's go," said Jane.

Dinner was great. Katie was like family. She got along with everyone. We talked and laughed and had fun.

After dinner, Katie and I volunteered to do the dishes. Everyone left us alone in the kitchen.

"I know you're mad about last night," Katie said, putting dishes in the dishwasher.

"I don't know that I'm mad, as much as I'm confused," I said, handing her more dishes.

"Confused about what? About our relationship?"

"Not necessarily. Confused about how you can flirt with guys right in front of me when you're drunk."

"But I was drunk. I didn't mean anything by it."

"I totally get that and thank you for saying that. But if you don't know what you're saying when you're drunk, you're going to get hurt sometime."

"How?"

"What if I'm not there? What if you go to a party at college and tell some guy you want to sleep with him? He won't know you're kidding, and if he didn't respect you, he'd take advantage of you. I would hate to know that happened."

"I see that," she said.

There was a minute of silence, as we finished the dishes.

"Wanna go for a walk?" I asked.

"Yes, let's go," Katie said.

We walked out the door hand in hand.

"I'm not mad," I repeated. "I just don't know how to act when you're drunk."

"Are you asking me not to drink?"

"No. That's your decision. I'm just not sure what we do or where we go from here."

"Are you thinking we should break up?" she said a little teary-eyed.

"No, I don't want that. I struggle with the drunk Katie, and I absolutely love the sober Katie."

"I love you too. And you can have both!"

"I want the sober Katie. I adore the sober Katie. I worry about the drunk Katie."

"So, what if you didn't go to parties with me anymore?" she asked.

"I've thought of that. But I worry what might happen to you if I'm not there."

"It's not like I flirt with guys every time I'm drunk."

"It only takes once," I said.

She was quiet. She knew I was right.

"Katie, I love you. I'll take a bullet for you. I'll protect you whenever I'm with you. But I don't know that I want to go to drinking parties with you and yet, I can't help you if I'm not there. I'm so conflicted."

We walked in silence for a minute.

"Maybe the answer is that I'll go to less of those drinking parties," she said.

"Are you okay with that?"

"Yes. But when I do go to one, you can't come with me since it's hard for you."

"I'm good with that," I said.

Would that help? I don't know. Maybe it was a Band-Aid. And as my mom said, only time will tell.

CHAPTER 12

OUR NEW RELATIONSHIP

For a few weeks, things were fine. I only saw the sober Katie, whom I loved. And as far as I knew, she only went to a couple EDM parties.

That helped me a lot, and the two of us were back to things being great. But was it a healthy relationship if we avoided the one thing that we disagreed upon? I think we both knew it was just a matter of time before it was going to come up again. But for the moment, we were happy and just focused on that.

I kept planning dates every Friday and Saturday to keep her away from the parties. I tried to make them fun so she wouldn't have any desire to go to the parties.

For one date, I hung a sheet in the backyard, and we got a movie projector and binge watched some old romance movies sitting in lounge chairs—one of her favorite things. Another fun date was when we cooked a gourmet meal together and then ate it by candlelight afterward. That was great fun to make it together and it was delicious.

We've done group dates playing games and going to escape rooms. We also had a beach night where we made a bonfire, roasted marshmallows, and made S'mores. They were so fun. Every date with the sober Katie was a blast.

But after a couple months, I heard from friends at school that she was going to parties after I dropped her off. Susan and Sarah had parties at their homes almost every weekend – and Katie was going to most of them.

One Sunday after family dinner, we went on another walk, and I had to talk about it.

"So have you been going to more parties?" I asked, already knowing the answer.

"Ah, yes," she said. "I've gone to some for the past couple weekends."

"Thanks for being honest with me."

"Are you upset?"

"No, I'm not upset. I just don't want anything to happen to you."

"I wish you would join me."

Silence...

"I know you're not the type to break the rules, but you could bend them every so often," she said.

I grinned. "Katie, is it going to bother you if I never drink?"

"I don't think so," she said. "It's just that I wish we could share that experience together, and I realize you don't want that part of me."

"I don't like that part of you. It's not you. You're so different when you're drunk."

"But what if you came with me, and we left before I got drunk?"

"How do we know when you've reached that point?"

"I'm not sure... but are you saying you'd do that for me?"

"Perhaps. If we can determine at what point we should leave. You're not trying to get me to drink, are you?"

"No."

"Good. Because I am not ready to change."

"But haven't you ever wondered what it would taste like?"

"Yes, I've wondered, but I don't need it. I've seen drinking cause the death of my grandparents, and I see what it does to you. Neither is something that makes me want to start drinking."

"I get that. The next time there's a party, I'll let you know. If you want to go, we'll only stay an hour, and I'll only have one drink. Fair?"

"Fair," I agreed.

Katie was happy with the outcome of our talk. Her girlfriends were telling her I was a total drag on her fun. Especially Susan. They had been nit picking her for weeks, and in spite of it, Katie kept going to the parties and hearing it repeatedly.

So, that night was a small victory for Katie.

And truth be told, I knew Katie wasn't going to slow down her drinking.

She and her girlfriends were planning a trip to Mexico after graduation. The four of them had done pretty much everything together since kindergarten. Susan, Sarah, and Kellie probably told Katie that their trip would give her the chance to drink without worrying about offending me.

The legal drinking age in Mexico was 18, but the girls were worried that some bars would not serve 18-year-old Americans.

Kellie had a friend that made fake ID's and they all got them, so they'd be sure they were able to drink freely in Mexico. One day after school, Katie asked me to grab her wallet out of her purse. As I did, I opened it and flipped through credit cards, joking about going shopping with her, and I saw the fake ID.

I knew right away what it was.

"Give me that," she said with a laugh.

"Wow, I've never seen a fake ID before," I said. "It looks real."

"You're not mad?" she said.

"I'm impressed with your creativity," I said. "But I hope you don't get busted."

"The legal drinking age is 18 in Mexico, but Kellie said we should get them just in case," she said.

I didn't know how to feel about the fake ID. I knew she was going to drink there, but I was surprised they got fake IDs as an insurance plan to make sure there was nothing standing in their way.

Honestly, it made me question our relationship a little more. We seemed to be dancing around a major issue that I don't think either of us was going to change.

That night I went home and talked to my parents about it. My parents said that I was letting my emotions overtake what I knew was right.

"Sometimes we confuse what is easy with what is right," my dad said. "But they are often not the same thing. It's easy to stay together. But maybe if you step away from the situation for a while and really give it some thought and prayer, you'll get the right answer," he said.

"Are you saying I should break up with her?" I said.

"Not necessarily," dad said. "I'm saying give it some time away and that will help you decide."

"You've heard the saying 'absence makes the heart grow fonder' Jake?" mom said.

"Yes."

"Maybe being apart for a while will help you decide how and if you want your relationship to continue."

"But it's the last month of school, and we are going to prom and then we have graduation," I said.

"You don't have to take a break right now, but give it some thought. Sometimes it's hard to see the forest through the trees."

"I may do it, but if I do, I may wait until school is over," I said.

"You have to decide what you can live with and what you can't," dad said. "And while you can't expect her to change for you, you'll need to decide if your differences are something you can live with, or if you want to change for her, or if you can't. Time will tell."

"Thanks. Love you guys."

"We love you too, Jake. And we're sure you'll do the right thing."

That night, I went to bed early, but went to sleep late. For hours, I thought about Katie and our relationship. Could I live with her drinking? Should I change my commitment so we can get over this situation and be happy? Do I want to drink? Maybe my commitment was made when I was too young and naïve...

All these and more thoughts kept going through my head. But my thoughts kept going back to how much I loved Katie. She was fun and kind and made me so happy. We laughed a lot. I loved how she respected everyone—even if they were totally opposite than she was. She helped people. She wasn't afraid to be goofy and yet, she was one of the most classy and sophisticated girls I'd ever known. She was everything I ever wanted in a girlfriend.

So, was I wrong for letting one thing stand in the way of our happiness? Should I change for her?

I struggled with those questions all night but found absolutely no answers to them. Trying to determine if our relationship was going to work or not was agonizing.

I thought of how much our relationship had changed since our first date in the Greek restaurant after practice. She was "my little project," but now my little project was presenting big questions about our future. It hurt my head trying to figure out what to do.

The next day, I woke to a news report about a major earthquake and tsunami in Brazil that destroyed dozens of cities and killed tens of thousands of people.

My mom was in tears watching it on TV. "It's so sad," she said.

"Mom, is it another sign of the end of the world like we learned in church?" Jane asked.

"It might be," mom said. "We need to say a prayer for the people of Brazil."

I texted Katie. "*Did you hear about the earthquake in Brazil?*"

"*Yes, how devastating,*" she texted.

"*It's another sign of the times,*" I texted. "*There have been so many of them this year.*"

"*I agree. I'm so sad for those people. I need a big hug from you today,*" she texted.

"*You got it. Love you,*" I texted.

"*Love you too. See you soon.*"

In addition to my mind being consumed with what to do in my relationship, I somehow made room in there to ponder the end of the world too. The end of the world and Second Coming don't scare me. I know it's part of the plan. If I let my emotions get the best of me, it could really bother me. However, I wanted to stay focused on helping others get through these times.

At school, everyone was talking about the earthquake. There was so much sadness. It was like a dark cloud hovering over everyone.

Radical sackcloths were telling students that they needed to repent because the world was approaching an end soon. They walked down the hall and yelled, "Repent ye, repent ye, for the end is near!"

While we all need to repent, their message took away from the sadness we were feeling for the people who lost their lives.

I saw Katie after fourth period, and she gave me a big hug in the hall and didn't let go.

"How are you holding up?" I asked.

"It's so sad. There's over 30,000 people dead," she said. "And they're still counting. It could be worse," she said with a tear in her eyes.

"I know. It's so hard to understand," I said. "But we have to be strong to support others."

"Can you come over after school?" she asked. "I really need some Jake time today—you help calm my heart."

"Of course. I'll meet you by your locker after school," I said.

The rest of the day went slowly because everyone was so sluggish and down about the tragedy--everyone except for the sackcloths who were acting like there was no tragedy. Their cries to "Repent!" were getting old.

In my student government class, Ms. Parker was also affected by the earthquake and massive deaths.

"I want to talk about what happened in Brazil today, instead of planning the prom," Ms. Parker said. "Are we far enough along on planning prom that we can take a break from it today?" she asked.

"Yes, Ms. Parker, I think we're caught up on everything," I said. "And it's more important that we discuss what happened today."

"OK. The details are there were 15 earthquakes and dozens of aftershocks in southeastern Brazil. The 15 ranged from a 6.4 to a 9.8—which are some of the biggest earthquakes ever recorded. Those triggered tsunami's that caused massive flooding. The death toll is currently estimated at more than 38,000, but it will take weeks to count the dead."

"Let's talk about how we deal with this. Let's start with questions you might have," she said.

"How can we be happy knowing so many people died?" Ashton asked.

"Do you think there will be more earthquakes?" Cindy asked.

"One at a time," Ms. Parker said. "First the question about happiness. It is normal to be sad when you hear of tragedies like this. If any of you have had a relative die, you know this feeling. And I think the body needs to mourn in order to heal."

"Ms. Parker, can I say something?" I asked.

"Yes, of course Jake."

"My grandparents died a few years ago in a tragic accident. It was devastating and my whole family was sad for months. It hurts for a while; I'm not going to lie. But it gets easier over time. You have to realize that their spirits live on, and you have to make the best of every day you have left on earth."

"That's beautiful Jake," Ms. Parker said.

"I agree with Jake," Chandler said. "I think we should honor those people who died by trying to make the best of every day. That doesn't mean we just forget them and be happy. But we need to remember that for us, life goes on and we should do good things for others in their memory."

"Do you think there will be more earthquakes?" Cindy asked again.

"It's quite possible," Ms. Parker said. "And with our history of earthquakes here in California, it's possible we'll have some too."

"I have a question," said Stephanie.

"OK, go ahead," Ms. Parker said.

"If there was a God, wouldn't He stop things like this?"

"What does everyone think?" Ms. Parker said.

"Here's my opinion," I said. "Stephanie, there most definitely is a God. But His plan isn't to stop every bad thing that happens: every accident, every death, every disaster. If we never experienced sorrow, the times of joy and happiness wouldn't be as happy. We grow stronger from the bad things that happen to us. Tougher. More compassionate and understanding. Just look at us all today—we're sitting around talking about our feelings, and here in this room, there's a definite feeling of love that we have for each other. That would not happen if everything today was the same as yesterday."

"OK, I get that," Stephanie said.

Class was deep today with a lot of loved shared and tears shed among everyone. When the bell rang, I was excited to see Katie and go to her house, so I rushed to the door.

"Jake, can you stay for a minute?" Ms. Parker asked.

"Busted!" said Chandler as he headed out the door.

"Sure. What do you need?" I asked.

"I want to thank you for your answers today. I admire how grounded you are and the things you said were very mature, helpful answers that the other students needed to hear. Thank you."

"Happy to help."

I headed toward Katie's locker. She was already there when I got there.

"How are you doing?" I asked.

"It's been a rough day," she said. "Can we just hang out at my house and snuggle up on the couch for a bit?"

"Yes, that sounds good. My brain needs a rest from all the emotions," I said.

She closed her locker, grabbed my hand, and we walked down the hall toward the parking lot.

When we got to her Hummer, I smiled when I saw her bumper sticker. I opened the door for her.

"Thank you," she said. "I'll see you at my place."

"OK."

As I got into my car, I was still thinking about the earthquake in Brazil, the emotions that everyone had that day, the possibility that this was another sign of the end of the world, and where my relationship was headed with Katie. It was a lot to process.

I only spent 30 seconds thinking of each topic, and I was already pulling into Katie's driveway.

When I got out, she grabbed my hand and we walked into her house.

"Hi Hannah," I said.

"Oh, hi Jake. Hi honey," she said to me and Katie. "What a sad day today, huh?"

"Yes. It's been like a dark cloud hanging over everyone all day," Katie said.

"I'm so sorry," Hannah said.

"We're going to sit in the family room for a bit, Mom," Katie said.

As we sat on the couch and snuggled up to each other, she leaned her head on my shoulder. I loved that.

"How can we be happy with life after such a tragedy?" she said.

"Our whole student council class was spent talking about the disaster and how everyone felt," I said. "It was very good to get things out. Maybe we should talk through things."

"Yeah, I'd like that. OK, how do we deal with this?"

"One of the things we talked about in student council was how we dealt with other deaths in our lives. It's sad. It's supposed to be. And it takes a while to get over it. But in time, we can get over it and be happy again."

"I guess so."

"I told the class about my grandparents—that is was devasting for my whole family. But over time, you realize that life has to go on and you have to make the best of every day."

"Jake?"

"Yes?"

"I love you," she said.

"I love you too. But why did you say that?"

"Because you are right. This experience was totally tragic and sad, and it will hurt for a long time. But life must go on and we need to realize that we can help others along the way."

We sat on the couch for an hour and just held each other, knowing that our love was strong enough to get us through the sadness of that day.

CHAPTER 13

CHOICES

T he next day at school, things were only a little better. There was still a gloomy overtone to everything.

During first period, Tyson seemed more upset than the day before.

"You ok man?" I asked.

"I think so," he said.

But I could tell he was still bothered by the earthquake.

After class I walked out with him. "What's up man?"

"I'm in trouble," Tyson said.

"What? How?"

He was silent.

"What did you do?"

He couldn't speak.

"Tyson, what's up? What kind of trouble are you in and how can I help?"

"You can't help," he said.

"Is it the earthquake?"

"No. It's Kami," he admitted.

"What's wrong?"

"She's pregnant," Tyson said quietly.

"Oh no. I'm so sorry."

"I found out last night. She had me and my parents come to her house... Really it was her parents that made me and my parents come to her house to tell us the news."

"Wow. I'm sorry man. How terrible was that?"

"Her parents tried to make me out to be the bad guy. My parents were mad at me but kept saying that it takes two people to have sex."

"She didn't accuse you of doing this against her will, did she?" I asked.

"No. Kami was cool and told them it was consensual. But I don't think her dad thought his little girl would ever do that."

"So, what's next? What are you two going to do?" I asked.

"I don't know. I'm too young to be a father. We're both too young to be parents."

"Her parents want her to get an abortion. But she would rather give it up for adoption," he said.

"What do you want?" I asked.

"I don't know. I'm not a fan of abortion, so maybe she should give it up for adoption," Tyson said.

"Wow. I'm blown away," I said.

"Thank you," he said.

"For what?" I asked.

"For not saying 'I told you so.' You told me a couple times to be careful and I didn't listen," he said. "I'm sorry I didn't listen" he said with a tear in his eye.

"I'm here for you man," I said.

"My life will be changed forever now. All because of one night. One choice. One stupid thing I did."

The bell rang for second period.

"I've gotta get to class. Are you going to be ok?" I asked.

"Yes, I'll be fine. It's like you say: you gotta make the best of the situation, right?"

"Of course. Let's talk more later. I will help however I can."

My mind was already filled with emotions about the earthquake, the end of the world, and my relationship with Katie. Now I added Tyson and Kami's pregnancy to it.

I can't imagine being a father at 18 years old. But I know kids do it and sometimes everything works out. I hoped for the best for Tyson but felt the pain he was going through.

The whole day was a big blur. The news of Kami's pregnancy was all over school by lunch. It kind of took kids minds off the tragedy in Brazil for a bit.

Radical sackcloths found out about Tyson and Kami and felt they needed to take action. The same group of radicals that were beating up that boy in September for being gay were waiting for Tyson after sixth period. Luckily, me and Chandler had sixth period with Tyson and walked out of class with him.

"Jenson!" one of the radicals yelled when they saw him.

"What?" he asked quietly.

"You defiled Kami Donahoe. Do you realize the punishment God will bring upon you?"

"Guys, I'm not interested in talking to you about this."

"Well, we're gonna talk about it," as he pushed Tyson into a locker.

I immediately jumped in and pulled the radicals off Tyson. Chandler stood next to Tyson to protect him.

"Guys, leave him alone," I said. "He's handling this on his own and does not need you to make it any worse."

"Get out of the way, Peterson. This isn't your issue."

"Yes, it is," I said loudly pushing him out of the way.

"You don't want this fight," Chandler said loudly. "Trust me!"

The radicals saw that me and Chandler were going to defend Tyson. The three of us could easily take the four of them, and they knew it.

"You're going to hell Jensen! Straight to hell," the head radical yelled, pointing his finger at Tyson.

"There are four fingers pointing back at you," Chandler said. "Now get the hell out of here or you're going to wish you never started this."

The radicals left. The crowd that had gathered to watch a fight followed.

Tyson was more emotional now knowing that he may have to defend himself against the radical sackcloths again. "Thanks guys," Tyson said. "I appreciate that."

"We're with you man," I said.

"Especially if you name the baby *Chandler*," Chandler said jokingly.

"Only if it's a girl," Tyson joked back.

Tyson had a few other run-ins with the radicals over the next two weeks, but every time, he was with us, and we protected him.

Kami's family decided to pull her out of school for the rest of the year to save any more embarrassment. Even though there were only two weeks left, they felt it was best.

After much discussion, they decided that they would let her give the baby up for adoption when she had it. Tyson agreed with the decision but didn't really have much of a say in it because of her parents. Kami's parents were relentless in blaming Tyson for her pregnancy, and they told her she was not to spend any more time with him. It really affected him for a while.

That Saturday night was prom. We had been planning it for the past three months in Ms. Parker's student council class. Like homecoming, I didn't have to do anything at the dance since I was going to it.

Since homecoming was spent with my friends, Katie and I agreed that prom would be spent with her friends. Luckily, Chandler asked Katie's friend Sarah to the prom, so that was great. Tyson didn't go. He didn't want to take anyone other than Kami and her parents didn't want her to be with him.

The day of prom, my car was not working again. Katie let me drive her Hummer. Mom drove me to her house that afternoon so I could pick up the Hummer. Driving her Hummer around was cool. I felt like I could drive over anything, and it wouldn't hurt the car at all. In fact, I could probably drive over a small sedan and not even feel it!

That night, I picked up Chandler, and we went to Sarah's house for pictures. I dropped him off at Sarah's and walked over to get Katie.

As I walked up to Katie's door, I thought of how crazy of a year it was for the two of us. I hoped that we would be able to stay close over these next couple weeks until she left for her trip to Mexico. Secretively, I was hoping she would not go to any drinking parties until Mexico, so she could see that we can be happy without that. I'm sure she hoped that we would go to those parties and that it would show me that I could be happy with it.

As I opened her door, Hannah was there to greet me. "Jake, you look so handsome," Hannah said.

"Thank you, Hannah. How are you doing?" I asked.

"Great. You two are going to have so much fun tonight."

Just as she said that, Katie walked downstairs in a long white prom dress with her hair done like a movie star and sparkly things in it.

"Wow! You look gorgeous!" I said.

She smiled. "Thank you. And you look so handsome in that black tux!"

"Shall we?" I asked, taking her arm.

"Why of course," she said as we walked out the door to Sarah's house.

"Can you believe school's out in two weeks?" she asked.

"This year flew by so fast," I said.

"So, we have to enjoy tonight," she said. "Let's make tonight fun, and happy and romantic and memorable."

"Yes. Definitely. A night to remember for the rest of our lives," I said.

At Sarah's house, everyone was there waiting on us.

Pictures were fun. Susan's parents hired a professional photographer who brought a variety of backdrops and had us pose in all sorts of funny poses. I dipped Katie like a ballroom dancer would. That was fun. Then we did a kissing photo—something I'm not fond of doing for a photographer. But Katie liked it.

We all went to dinner at The Chateau—a ritzy French restaurant that served some of the best food I'd ever tasted but also the smallest portions I've ever seen.

We talked about not being ready for graduation and college next fall. Everyone said the year flew by and we were all going to miss high school.

The dance was a blast. Chandler, Sarah, Katie, and I all danced together for most of the night. It was non-stop, loud music; a total blast. The last half hour of the dance was all slow songs, and that's when Katie and I could talk.

"I love you, Jake Peterson. Even if you never break the rules." She laughed.

"I love you too."

After a minute, I said, "What's going to happen to us after this school year? We're both going to different colleges and...."

"Shh," she said. "Remember when I said we were going to make tonight fun, memorable, and happy? Let's not talk about that tonight please."

"Got it. Then tell me this – what's the one thing you will remember most about us this year?"

"One thing? Wow, I don't know if I can only pick one... Hmmm. It might have to be the night you kissed me for the first time."

"Wait—It was YOU who kissed ME!" I said jokingly.

"Funny man. I'll never forget that night. It just was such a strong expression of love. I will always remember that.

"Good answer."

"But there are so many great memories of us. Football games, going out to Nielsons for ice cream, you coming to parties with me, me going to your family's Sunday dinners, the little project jokes... I could go on and on."

"Jake, I never knew I could feel so much love for someone. You are the type of guy every girl dreams of."

"Like a nightmare?" I joked.

"I'm serious. You're a total gentleman. You help everyone. You're kind and such a good person. Heck—have you ever broken any rules in your entire life?"

"Lots of them. But I'm the lucky one. You are so sweet and fun to be around. No one has ever made me happier than you have. And I'm a very happy person normally, but around you, I'm even more."

We kissed on the dance floor and everything and everyone else seemed to fade away for just a minute. Until Ms. Parker tapped me on the shoulder and said "Hey guys, remember there's no public display of affection tonight. Sorry."

I remembered. I was one of the ones that set that rule four months ago when we planned prom. "Sorry Ms. Parker," I said.

At the end of the dance, Katie and I were still in a romantic trance. I hoped it would continue through the night.

"Everyone ready for the after party at my place?" Susan asked.

There were cheers from everyone in our group. I hoped it didn't turn into a major drinking party. But that was an unrealistic expectation.

I promised Katie I would go for a while. And since we were in a happy mood, I thought we'd be ok.

But on prom night, some kids feel like the best way to make it memorable is to drink a lot.

Our prom group of eight were not the only people at Susan's house. She must have invited half the senior class. There were at least 100 kids at her house. Her house was wall-to-wall people. There was a lot of alcohol and almost everyone was drinking. Chandler wasn't much of a drinker, so he and I hung out for a while, when Sarah and Katie went to help Susan in the kitchen.

"Is this party going to ruin the night for you man?" Chandler asked.

"I sure hope not. We had a fun time at dinner and the dance," I said. "I just hope Katie doesn't get drunk."

Chandler knew of our issues with drinking as he and I talked about everything.

"Man, just be cool and let things happen. If she gets out of hand, we can always leave," Chandler said.

"I don't know if I could leave her, knowing how she acts when she's drunk."

"But Jake, you're not her parent and you're not her husband. She's 18, and she can make her own decisions," Chandler said.

"Understood," I said pondering what I would do if Katie got too drunk.

"It's been like 30 minutes. Let's find the girls," he said.

"Yes," I agreed, and we searched the house for Katie and Sarah.

There were people everywhere. What started as a big party had grown even bigger. There were people in every room of Susan's house and in the back yard.

As we went looking for the girls, we were greeted by everyone. That slowed us down another 20 or 30 minutes in our search to find them.

We eventually found them in the living room. Sarah was sitting next to some guy and Katie was sitting on a guy's lap.

"Dude—do you see that?" Chandler asked.

"Yes. I think you're going to see the drunk Katie," I said, feeling like the emotional bond we felt an hour ago was gone.

"What's going on, girls?" Chandler asked.

Sarah jumped up and hugged Chandler. "Where have you been?" she asked him. "I haven't seen you in a long time."

"We were out back waiting for you two," he said.

Katie was still sitting on the lap of a guy I'd never seen before, who was likely from another school.

"Are you ok, Katie?" I asked, trying to see if she'd get up.

"I'm so good Jake," she said slurred.

"Who's your friend?" I asked.

"I don't know," she said. "He goes to Central. He gave me a drink, and I don't remember much since then."

"Did you spike her drink?" I asked, ready for a fight.

"No man, I just handed her a drink from the bar. It was whiskey," he said. "She drank it all, and it must have made her drunk really fast. Who are you anyway?"

"I'm her boyfriend."

"If you're her boyfriend, why is she sitting on my lap?" he asked, pushing Katie off his lap and stood up like he was ready to fight me.

"Hold on man," Chandler said jumping between us. "If she's drunk and doesn't remember anything, that's not fair. Katie and Jake have been together the entire school year. They went to prom tonight."

He could see I was mad, and I was bigger than him. "OK. No worries man. She came onto me. She asked if she could sit on my lap." He put his hands up as if to say *Don't hit me, I'll go.* "Sorry man. But I wouldn't have thought she had a boyfriend because she was flirting with me. I apologize," he said, walking away.

"Thank you," I said.

"Katie, we should take you home," I said.

"Not yet, the party is just getting started," she said.

"Don't be a party pooper, Jake," Sarah said.

"Katie, remember our talk about leaving the party when you've had too much? Well, you've had too much."

"Jake, I'm not leaving. Maybe you should leave," she said slurring her words. ⸱

I wasn't hurt by that because I knew she didn't mean it. But I was torn. Do I stay and watch drunk Katie flirt with any guy she meets? Do I leave the party and hope she ends up safe? I didn't know what to do.

"Katie and I are spending the night at Susan's house after the party, so you don't need to worry about anything Jake," Sarah said.

Chandler could see I was conflicted. "Maybe we should just go home. She'll be ok if she's staying here tonight."

"Go home Jake," Katie said. "Let me have my fun."

I looked at Katie for a second, trying to see if she'd change her mind.

"OK, Chandler, let's go," I said.

"You ok if I get him out of here?" Chandler asked Sarah.

"Yes, of course. Thank you for such a fun evening," Sarah told Chandler.

"Me too," he said giving her a quick kiss.

"Katie, be safe, ok?"

"I'm fine Jake."

I felt like I was doing the wrong thing to leave, but I also felt like I would be doing the wrong thing if I stayed. Either way I was wrong. I'd never felt that way before—there's usually a right choice and a wrong choice. But that night, I felt like there was no right choice.

I drove Chandler home in Katie's Hummer.

"I can't believe what she did tonight Chandler," I said. "Why is it that every time she's drunk, she becomes a big flirt? She's not a big flirt when she's sober."

"I don't know man," Chandler said. "Alcohol affects people in different ways. It sucks that she becomes a big flirt when she's drunk."

"Why couldn't she become tired and sleepy when she's drunk? I could live with that much easier."

"I don't know man. Cool off tonight and go see her tomorrow."

"Good night man," I said as I dropped him off.

I felt like my relationship with Katie was the poster child for bi-polar couples. We were as hot as fire when she was sober, and as cold as ice when she was drunk. The whole way home I kept thinking about what to do.

I remembered my parent's advice of giving it time and maybe even giving us some distance for a while. A few weeks ago, distance was the last thing I wanted. Now, I felt like that was the best advice.

CHAPTER 14

MAKING MY CHOICE

After spending most of the night and all morning pondering what to do about our situation, I texted Katie Sunday afternoon asking when I could bring the Hummer to her.

"Come any time. I want to see you," she texted back.

"Great. I'll head over now."

As I drove to her house, I wasn't sure what I was going to say. I didn't have any idea of how to respond to her actions last night, and I was unsure about how we go on with our relationship. I felt like a soldier going into battle without a plan or a weapon. I was vulnerable, but I didn't care. I knew that talking things out was the only way we'd resolve this.

When I pulled in her driveway, she was sitting on her front porch waiting for me. She had a concerned look on her face. She ran up to me, threw her arms around me and said "I am so sorry for what I did last night Jake. I love you!"

"I love you too. Do you remember what you did and what you said to me?"

"Not totally. But Sarah texted me this morning," she said. "I really sat on some strange guy's lap? And I really told you to go home?"

"Uh huh," I said.

"Wow. Jake, I'm sorry. That was obviously the alcohol talking and not my true feelings."

"I know. But that's what worries me. You want to drink with your friends, but you get drunk fast, don't know what you're doing, and become a big flirt. What if I didn't find you when I did? That guy wanted you, Katie. He wanted to take advantage of you."

"I'm sorry Jake. We need a change."

"Yes," I said, thinking she was going to tell me she was going to stop drinking.

"I like drinking. I like the social aspect of it, and I like that I connect with my girlfriends when I drink with them. Jake, I mean no disrespect to your grandparents, but you've avoided alcohol for a lot of years since they died. Perhaps it's been long enough."

"Seriously?" I said.

"Perhaps you can still honor them by drinking responsibly. I want to be with you. And I want us to be together always. But I think you should consider that nearly all adults drink and I'm inviting you to do that with me, on your time, at your own pace."

"Wow. I never expected you to ask me to change who I am for you, since I never would ask you to change who you are for me."

"Jake, you need to remember that we love each other. We're perfect for each other. I'm asking you to move on to adulthood by joining me in something that you'll eventually do anyway. You don't have to do it now. Not even next month. But sometime in the future."

"I don't know Katie," I said, not sure how to take all of that.

"I'm not asking you to make a decision today," she said. "Just think about it.

I don't want your answer until I get back from Mexico. That's three weeks from now. Especially when I'm gone, you should really think about it."

"OK," I said quietly.

"I have an idea," she said. "I think it would be good for both of us to use my week in Mexico as a week without any communication."

"What? Why?"

"I think we'll both be able to think clearer if we're not talking or texting or video chatting. You need a week without me bugging you, without the emotions of our relationship getting in the way of your thoughts."

Wow. Had she been talking to my parents?

"Ah... ok," I said. "Maybe a short time apart might help us think clearer."

"The way I see it, we're meant for each other. We should be together forever. So, take until the day I get back to make your decision. And remember that I love you more than anything, Jake Peterson!"

I tried to respond, but she put her finger over my lips to stop me. "Please no more discussion today. Please do that for me," she said.

With those eyes and the way she smiled at me, I'd agree to almost anything. I swallowed hard and agreed to wait. She wasn't changing...And I really had to do some deep thinking to figure out what I wanted.

We hugged in front of her Hummer, and I glanced at the bumper sticker I gave her.

My little project was giving me an ultimatum. Be more accepting of something I didn't agree with or break up.

The next five days were easy in preparation for finals, but the following five days were the last days of school, and they were rough with final exams each day. Katie and I spent some time studying together, but we didn't have any classes together, so we didn't see each other a lot.

We went on a date the night before graduation with the agreement that there was no talk about drinking or the decision she wanted me to make.

That date was pure bliss. I took her paddle boarding and snuck dinner along, so we had a paddle board picnic. It was peaceful and beautiful and gave us time to enjoy each other.

How was it possible that I was so in love with Katie Martin every minute of every day until she drank alcohol? We were so happy together. We joked and laughed. We cared so much about each other.

That night when I dropped her off, I told her that I couldn't imagine my life without her. I think my family would be mad at me if we ever broke up, especially Jane.

Graduation was the next morning at 11:00. Katie's flight to Mexico left at 4 P.M. In a way, I was looking forward to the break because my head had been spinning for weeks.

As senior class president, I had to be there early because I was giving one of the speeches at graduation.

We had graduation at the auditorium at the local college. I showed up a little earlier than I was supposed to because I needed to sit in silence for a bit and clear my head. Ms. Parker and our principal Mrs. Evans were the only ones there.

"Hi Jake, are you ready?" Ms. Parker said.

"Yes, I think so," I said.

"Are you nervous?" Mrs. Evans asked.

"No, why? Do I look nervous?"

"No. But you're here 20 minutes before you're supposed to be," Mrs. Evans said.

"I needed a little quiet time to go through my speech again."

"Good idea. We'll leave you alone," Ms. Parker said. And the two of them went off to get ready.

I read through my speech a couple times. I felt ready. So, I sat and absorbed the situation. I thought about the closure that graduation brings to high school. I thought about my four years there and how much I've grown. And I thought about senior year, and the happiness I had with Katie.

Today was the end of a chapter in my life, and I wanted to take it all in.

I watched as other speakers showed up to sit on the stage with me one by one. Everyone seemed more nervous than I was. Maybe I wasn't taking this serious enough, I thought.

Susan Johnson sat by me. She was speaking after me.

"Are you nervous?" she asked.

"Not really. You?"

"Terrified."

"You'll do well once you get going. You always speak with energy and emotion. Just do that today and you'll be fine."

"Thank you, Jake. You're so kind."

The auditorium filled with parents and families quickly and before we knew it, it was 11 A.M. and time to start.

After the processional of students walking into the auditorium to the graduation march song, Principal Evans gave the introductory remarks. Honestly, I was zoned out for a bit because of the emotions of the moment.

My mind went to Katie and how I would ever make up my mind what to do. I wasn't sure a week was enough time to make my decision. Part of me wished I could call Katie just once during the week. But I also felt no communication could really be a good thing. My mind was racing through my thoughts, and I realized I was so conflicted...

Just then, Susan Johnson elbowed me. "Jake, it's your turn to speak."

The audience was applauding. My name was on the big screen behind the stage: *Jake Peterson, Senior Class President*

I jumped up and went to the podium.

"Seniors, teachers, families and fellow classmates, I welcome you to our graduation ceremonies. I've been asked to speak today because I served as senior class president this year. But I want to speak to you today as your friend and fellow graduate."

"Give 'em hell Jake!" someone in the audience yelled to a round of laughter.

"I think we've all learned a lot this year. And not only in our classes. Oh, those were great. And we appreciate all the teachers for their efforts. But I think there were many life lessons learned this year by all of us. We realized there are a lot of problems in the world. There is a lot of anger, hatred, and fighting. We observed it around the world, and we even experienced it in our school."

"But one thing I learned this year, is that we need to set aside our differences and get along. There is no happiness in conflict. There is no happiness in doing the wrong things. And there is no hope in expecting everyone to be the same. We are not all the same and never will be. Just because someone has extreme opposite views than you do, does not make them wrong. Just because you feel strongly about your views does not mean your views are the only right ones."

"You tell 'em Jake!" someone yelled.

"We all seek happiness. I've learned that the only way to be truly happy is to love everyone and respect everyone and not try to change everyone who doesn't believe what you believe. Because at the foundation of everyone's character, we all come from the same God in Heaven. Think of it. God made us all. That makes us all brothers and sisters. Really."

"Before our political affiliation, before our alliance to a school or team, before anything else that makes us who we are and what we believe in, we are all made of God. I would suggest that happiness comes from realizing that everyone is special, accepting differences and showing love, not anger."

"Amen," a few people said, as if we were in church. Others laughed at that.

"We can be happy despite politics, despite world disasters and devastation, despite problems and all the bad things that happen to us in life. So as your friend and classmate, my wish for everyone is happiness. True happiness. And that comes by caring about others more than ourselves. It comes by helping people in need. It comes by making good choices in life and being a friend to all. If you remember one thing from this year, from this graduation ceremony, I hope you remember that you are in charge of your own happiness for the rest of your life. Yes, other people and other events can influence how you react, but you get to choose if you're happy or not."

"So, choose happiness. Choose to love and not hate. Choose to be a friend to kids who don't have many friends and do things for people who might be down on their luck. I have loved my years at West View High School. Thank you to all our teachers and staff who have served us. To my fellow graduates and all of you, I hope that you will find happiness for the rest of your lives. Thank you."

There was immediate applause when I finished. It grew louder. And then it turned into a standing ovation. There were cheers and clapping and a feeling of energy that came over the audience.

I was humbled at the response. Perhaps with as many problems the world had, the people in attendance needed a reminder about happiness too.

At the end of the ceremony, Principal Evans read the names of every student in alphabetical order to come up and receive their diploma. She asked the audience to not cheer or clap until the end, but does any family ever hold back?

When she read Katie's name, I even clapped and cheered. I was really going to miss her this week.

When she read my name, I felt a rush of energy going through me and I jumped up and went through the line to get my diploma.

"Jake, your speech was wonderful," Mrs. Evans said.

I hugged her, thanked her, and then walked down the long aisleway to the exit. I heard my family cheering for me as I walked out. I took it all in, knowing that high school was over, and my life would be changing forever.

Out in the parking lot where students gathered waiting for their families, I first saw Chandler.

"Dude! We did it!" I said, hugging him.

"Your speech moved me man," Chandler said. "Thank you for what you said. You taught us a life lesson today."

"Thanks man."

"Jake my boy!" Tyson shouted as he came over to us.

It was good to see him smile. After all the issues with getting Kami pregnant, he hadn't been himself for a while.

"Can you believe it?" I asked.

"I'm so glad it's over," Tyson said. "It's been a hell of a year."

"Hey, where's Ben?" Chandler asked.

"He's over there talking with Susan Johnson," Tyson said.

"Maybe she has the hots for him," Chandler said to a round of laughter.

There was a big celebration in the parking lot. There were hugs, kisses, and lots of selfies.

My family found me in the crowd.

"Jake your speech was phenomenal," mom said.

"Yeah, it moved everyone," dad said. "Let's get a family picture."

"Chandler, will you take a few pics for us?" mom asked.

As we were posing for family pics, the crowd thinned out a bit. And that's when I saw Katie.

"Katie, come over and get in this photo with us," my sister Jane said.

"Yes, please Katie," echoed my mom.

"OK," she said as she snuggled right up to me.

After way too many photos, I needed some time alone with her. Yes, we were in the parking lot with hundreds of people. But she was leaving in a couple hours to go to the airport, and I needed to be with her for just a minute.

We held hands as we walked toward the edge of the parking lot where her Hummer was parked. As soon as we got close to her car, she stopped and hugged me. She squeezed me hard.

"Your speech was great," she said.

"Thank you."

"I mean it. How do you always seem to say what people need to hear?" she asked.

"I will miss you so much."

"I'll miss you too," I said kissing her.

"I can't wait to hear your decision when I get back." She gave me that smile that would melt anyone's heart.

I looked back at her like a hypnotized fool. "I know."

"It will be like a scene from the movies," she said.

"Oh yeah?" I asked.

"After a week apart, a week of reflection, a week without any communication, you will realize you can't live without me and that we can be happy as long as we're together—regardless of what we do. So, you're going to come to my house next Saturday afternoon—don't come in the morning, as I'll still be tired—and we're going to run into each other's arms and hug and kiss and start a new life together."

"You have it all figured out," I said.

"Yes, I do. Jake, I will miss not hearing from you for a whole week. But we are made to be together, and we can get through this one week to strengthen our relationship."

"I agree."

She kissed me again. "I look forward to seeing you next Saturday. Just remember to run into my arms and kiss me big!"

"Yes ma'am," I said giving her another kiss.

She turned and walked away, and that started our week of radio silence.

Never had I been so conflicted about any decision. This was Katie Martin—the most perfect girl in the world. She was smart, funny, and amazing in every way. She was asking me not only to be comfortable with her drinking socially, but to eventually join her. "Becoming an adult" as she said.

On one hand, I wasn't being asked to change my stance on drinking—I was only being asked to be with her as she drank.

On the other hand, I knew that if I went through with it, eventually she would want me to drink.

My mind told me that logically, this was an easy decision... that if I wasn't going to change my stance on drinking, I should break up and move on. But my heart told me that Katie and I are so right for each other that I didn't want to risk the chance of losing her.

Maybe it was ok to bend the rules every so often... And maybe I just needed to break them.

That night I talked to my parents about it again.

"She gave you an ultimatum?" my mom asked.

"Sort of," I said. "I guess so. She never said what the results would be if I did not want to allow drinking in my life and our relationship..."

"But don't you think if you decide it's not for you, that will effectively end your relationship?" dad asked.

"I guess you're right," I said. "What would you guys do?"

"It's not up to us," dad said. "It's what you can live with. What you can be happy with. And only you know that."

"That's the problem—I don't know. On one hand, we are so happy together and I honestly love her so much."

"And on the other hand?" mom asked.

"I don't know if I'll ever be totally comfortable with the person she becomes when she drinks. And I don't know that I feel good about drinking yet."

"The week without communication may clear your head, Jake," mom said. "Really give some thought to what you want in life and who you want to be."

"Ok. I will. My biggest question is if it's worth giving up the 99% of the Katie that I love, for the 1% of Katie that I don't."

"Yet her drinking is 100% of the problem," dad said.

"Take the week and keep pondering it in your head and your heart," mom said.

"Thanks, you guys. You always have good advice," I said.

"With Katie gone this week, maybe you should get that work done on your car," dad said. "It's been giving you problems for months. Are you ok with that?"

"Yes, please!" I said. "It has been too long."

"Great. I'll call the shop tomorrow and see if we drop it off on Monday."

Being without a car for a week and sharing the family car was going to be a major inconvenience to me and my parents as well. But it needed to be fixed for a while, and since Katie was gone, I wouldn't likely be driving anywhere.

I spent the whole week thinking about my decision. Thinking about how much I loved her, how much fun we had, and the fact that I loved almost everything thing about her.

I still loved her when she was drunk, but she showed a side of herself that wasn't really her. It was a flirty and dangerous side. The more I thought about it, the more I kind of liked that she had a little dark side. If that was 50% of who she was, I probably wouldn't date her. But it was a measly 1%.

Every night all week my mind raced through thoughts like these and more. I talked to Chandler, Ben, and Tyson separately and got their opinion. They all reminded me it was my decision. They also all told me separately they had never seen me happier than when I was with Katie.

That was true.

One night, I thought about my grandparents and the commitment I made to not drink in their honor. Had I given them enough time without drinking to show them I honored them? Could I move on? Was my commitment to them the only reason I didn't drink? Would I refrain from drinking if they were still alive because of the person I am?

I took nearly every minute of every day to come to a conclusion. It wasn't until the day Katie was coming home that I made
my decision.

CHAPTER 15

MY KATIE CONNECTION

O nce I made my decision, the next step was to let Katie know. I decided to put my thoughts on a card and deliver it with a red rose. Although we agreed that we would not see each other until tomorrow, I didn't think there was anything wrong with delivering the message tonight before she got home.

My plan was to drive to her house around 7:30 and leave the card and rose in her room and be out by 8:00. She would be home a little after nine.

I mowed the lawn and took a shower before dinner. When I got out of the shower, my parents were gone. I texted them, and they had gone to dinner and left pizza for us—a common occurrence on a Friday night.

Friday was date night for them. I remember when I was younger thinking it was weird that my parents still went on dates. But now that I'm older, I realize parents need time together to remember they love each other without the stress of the kids.

After we ate all the pizza, I locked myself in my room and began to write my note to Katie. I had rehearsed in my mind a dozen times what I was going to say, but it was still challenging to put words on paper.

Once I finished, I had a great sense of relief to be done writing my answer. I had asked my mom if she'd pick me up a red rose when she went to the grocery store earlier, and she had it waiting in the fridge for me, so I was ready to go. I just needed wheels.

My car was still at the repair shop. I was planning on using my parent's car, but they were still out, and when I texted them, they said they would not be getting back until about nine. I texted my friends and no one was available to take me or let me borrow their car. It was too far to walk or run.... After 20 minutes of trying, I realized I had to find another way to get there and fast. So, I put the rose and card in a backpack and got on my bike.

I didn't mind riding the bike there, but I was in jeopardy of being late and running into Katie coming home before I left.

I got on my bike and rode faster to get there and back before she got home.

The whole way over to Katie's house, I debated if I should take the Connector Road or not. I avoid it most of the time, but that night, I needed to get to Katie's house before she got home, I was late and, on a bike, so I had to take it.

I didn't realize how late the bike would make me. Even though I rode fast, I didn't get to Katie's house until almost 8:30. Katie's mom met me at the door with a big hug.

"Katie's flight landed on time and she's on her way home," Hannah said.

"Oh, that's great," I said getting nervous about the timing.

"Do you want to wait for her?" Hannah asked. "She should be home in about 20 minutes."

"No thank you. I'd like this to be a surprise," I said.

"Oh nice," she said.

She filled a small vase with water and gave it to me so I could put the rose in it. She let me into Katie's room to set up my flower and card. I looked around Katie's room and saw so many things to remind her about us—one of my football jerseys, a bunch of pics of us, her prom corsage flowers hanging upside down to dry out, and more. We spent so much of our senior year together, I thought.

I tried to move quickly so I could leave without seeing her tonight. I put the flower in the vase and tried to stand up the card against the vase, but it kept sliding down. After a few attempts, I got the card to stand up and then was ready to go so I'd be gone before Katie got home.

Hannah took a picture of it and texted it to Katie, so she'd know my answer was there waiting for her.

But despite my attempt to leave quickly, Hannah—who adored me—wanted to visit for a minute. I was taught to show good manners and to respect adults, so I talked a little longer. We talked about the fun Katie had on her trip—which I didn't know anything about since we were on radio silence for the past week according to our agreement. Sounds like it was a big party the whole time. Given my decision about her, I was now ok with that.

I was listening to Hannah talk about the trip, but not really paying attention as I wanted to get out of there before Katie got home.

I looked at my phone and it was 8:44 already. I knew Katie was getting really close to home, so I excused myself. She asked again if I wanted to wait for Katie, but I told her I needed to get home.

"My brother and sister are home tonight, and I promised to watch them," I said, trying to get her to let me go.

"OK then," she said. "See you soon."

"Thanks Hannah."

I dashed out the door and got on my bike as quickly as possible. And because I didn't want Katie to see me on my way, I decided to take the Connector back home, knowing she avoided it all the time since her accident with the deer.

The sky was dark by the time I left Katie's house. I realized wearing black clothes and a black helmet was not very smart for riding my black bike at night. I rode faster, so I could get to the end of the Connector and onto a lighted street.

The evening was warm and calm, with only a few stars in the sky. I loved the feeling of the air on my face that kept me cool while riding fast. I could hear crickets as I drove along the old farm road. I wondered how many thousands were in the fields. But my focus quickly returned to getting onto the main road.

Sometimes when you've been warned enough times about dangerous situations, your mind starts to play tricks on you. That's what happened to me as I rode. I rode near the middle of the road to avoid the gravel on the edges, which if I slipped, would send me down into the ditch. I also kept envisioning deer running across the road, right into me, since that happened a lot on that road. The image of a deer knocking me off my bike made me chuckle a bit.

"That's ridiculous," I thought. "Stay focused."

The steepness of the hill made it hard to see the lights of oncoming cars until they went over the top and were driving down the other side. As I rode, I had heard a car approaching but couldn't see it over the crest of the hill. By the time I saw the lights, they were past the middle of the road and coming right at me.

Reacting quickly, I moved as far to the right edge of my lane as I could, to avoid the car without riding into the ditch.

But it wasn't far enough. The oncoming car came toward me quickly. As it came over the hill and got closer, I saw a pink bumper sticker "Jake's little project." It stunned me and I paused right in the middle of the road.

Katie.

Then, her speeding SUV hit me head on. She didn't even see me. She came over the top of the hill so fast, I couldn't move over far enough or fast enough. I couldn't escape the hit.

The impact of the hit ripped my helmet off my head. Her front bumper hit my head so hard it cracked my skull in half, launching me and my bike off the road, down into the ditch on the side, killing me instantly.

Katie didn't stop. She drove away, leaving me dead in the ditch on the side of the road in the dark of the night.

CHAPTER 16

BODY AND SPIRIT

The whole thing happened so quickly that I didn't even realize I was dead. I thought I blacked out. In just a split second, massive amounts of blood left my body, and I was done. Dead. Gone. Death is so quick that you don't realize it at first. When I opened my eyes, I felt pain-free.

I laid there trying to determine what just happened to me, wondering why I felt fine, when I knew I got hit by the SUV just seconds earlier. I felt no pain at all.

The transition from life to death is instantaneous. There's no warning. No announcement. No instructions on what's going to happen or what to do next. It happened so quickly, I didn't even have time to think about it.

The night was calm again—a stark contrast to what had happened just minutes ago. I could hear the crickets chirping in the distance. The sky was dark except for a few streetlights. And I was all alone.

My spirit hovered a couple feet above my dead body. I floated there, looking at my body for a while. The thought occurred to me that it might be God's way of helping me realize I really was dead.

As I floated over my body, I was sad, shocked, and peaceful all at the same time. So many emotions. I couldn't believe I was dead. I was too young. I expected to live forever. It all happened so fast. Literally, it took about two seconds, and I was gone. I never realized life was so fragile. I hadn't really thought about dying; what 18-year-old does?

I looked at my lifeless body covered in blood and my crushed bike. My skull had been crushed. Parts of my face were cut, and the skin was barely hanging on. Teeth were knocked out. Blood everywhere. I looked awful! It looked painful, but I didn't feel any pain. Just peace. I was shocked at the entire experience.

I floated in the air, staring at my dead body for what seemed like hours, inspecting the damage that was done by Katie's car. It was as if there were two of me—but the guy in the ditch didn't look so good.

Then, a myriad of questions ran through my head. What would my parents do? What about my family? And what would happen to Katie? She was the cause of my death. That's manslaughter. Katie... All these thoughts, and more, ran through my mind as I hovered above my body.

I wondered what would happen on earth without me, but I also looked at my lifeless body and felt a sense of closure to living on earth. It was surreal. I didn't even think about what was next because I was sad about the immediate end to my life.

How could this happen to me?

Why did I have to go now?

Why me?

I was too young. I had plans. Dreams. I wanted to change the world. Marry the girl of my dreams. And have kids of my own someday. Now, all of that was gone. Forever.

After observing my mangled, dead body for a while longer, the reality of the situation overwhelmed me. I wasn't going back. And that was emotionally painful.

I inspected my spirit. This was new to me. I was in the form of a ghost—not like something you see on TV, but me, glowing white. I had feelings but no body. My emotions were the biggest character trait I had in spirit form and practically the only one.

Floating was interesting and even fun. I was amazed how effortlessly I could float around and observe things. I tried floating backwards, sideways and in circles. All were equally amusing to me for just a moment.

After minutes of struggling with my death and floating around a bit, a peaceful feeling suddenly came over me. It was warm. It reassured me that this was part of some master plan. It was at that moment I realized I would be ok.

I also realized that I needed to move on to heaven.

Feelings are stronger when you're in spirit form. There are no addictions or cravings or physical pain to keep you from feeling a pure line of communication with Heaven.

I felt a source of power encouraging me to float upward toward heaven, not in an aggressive way, but in a very calm, welcoming way. Although I didn't know what was going to happen next, somehow, I knew floating upward was what I was supposed to do. And I knew that I should go when I was ready.

I got the feeling that God lets your spirit spend as much time floating over your body as you need to in order to deal with your death, and then He pulls you toward Him when you're ready.

When I realized there was no going back and I came to grips with the fact that my life was over, I bid farewell to my body and let my spirit float.

My spirit naturally went upward. I ascended slowly at first. As I floated, I could see the fields on both sides of the Connector. I could see the deer in the fields that might have distracted the girls in the car. There were dozens of them. I had control of my ascension, so along the way, I lingered in a few places.

I floated toward my house. When I saw it, I wondered how my parents would be without me. They are strong people, but would this be too hard to handle? I saw no signs of them being awake in the house. But I thought I would go into the house and see them. I floated near the house but somehow was stopped from being able to go in. I tried again, thinking I didn't guide my spirit right the first time, but despite my efforts to float into the house and see my family, I couldn't. The heavenly force that was pulling me upward wouldn't let me go into the house. At least not right now. I just had to view it from above.

I looked at the freshly mowed lawn that I had finished a few hours earlier. If I would have only known then what I know now, I would have waited to give Katie the news until tomorrow.

I saw the basketball hoop that I had spent hundreds of hours playing with my family and friends. I noticed the flowers that my mom planted every year that made our house look so nice.

I will miss that house. While it wasn't a mansion, our home was big enough for us, and it was filled with love. That's the most cherished memory of living there—that we all felt loved by great parents. I will miss that. I felt so much love for my parents and family, even more so now, knowing I would miss them deeply.

After floating around my house for a while, I felt I had to return to the task of ascending to heaven.

I let myself float upward again and admired my town from the sky. All the lights. The cars on the roads. My high school. The football field. From the sky, it was a magnificent view.

The night sky was so peaceful, and that had a calming effect on me.

After a few more minutes of floating around town, I finally gave in and let my spirit go upward again. Soon, I could see beyond our city to neighboring towns too. The lights from all the cities were dazzling.

My ascension began very slowly, as if to give me a chance to say goodbye to Bonita Del Sol. Higher and higher I went. It was like being in a helicopter, but without the helicopter noise.

As my spirit floated upward, I noticed the stars in the night sky. And a few clouds. The sky was calm. The irony in it all was that I felt very alive, and yet I was very, completely, and totally dead.

When I got to the point when the town was merely a speck below me, my ascension speed increased. It was an incredible feeling—not scary at all. I knew my spirit was going where it was supposed to, and I didn't have to direct it there; it went automatically. I laughed as I thought of what I was doing—floating above the earth toward heaven.

As my ascension increased in speed, I noticed other spirits in the distance floating upward as well. They had a glow about them too. None were very close to me—maybe the closest being a few miles away. There were spirits above me, to my left and my right. All were headed in the same direction. They might have been ascending with me the whole time, but until then, I had not noticed them.

I realized those were other people who had died that night just like me. And while they were too far away to see any details of them, I realized I was not alone in where I was going. I felt a connection to those spirits. I felt they were probably just as shocked as I was by the whole experience.

Earth looked spectacular, like photos from NASA: radiant and colorful. As I went along my path, I thought of how much had happened in the past couple hours – I'm dead, and now I'm floating toward heaven. It was surreal!

Once out of the view of earth, the night sky lightened a bit. Then, after a while further, I floated through a veil of white clouds. It was like a lining of thick, puffy clouds that took me out of our solar system into heaven. I was in the clouds for a while—they were so thick that I couldn't see through them. It was bright and airy, but because I couldn't see anything but white, I just let the ascension continue. I never felt claustrophobic, just comfortable.

Once I rose above that veil, the night sky instantly became brighter like someone flipped a switch and turned night into a sunny day. A very bright, sunny day!

At the point that I moved passed that veil, I remembered that I had been there before.

I remembered things about living in heaven before I came to earth: The plan to come to earth; the spirits who were my friends; the excitement we felt in heaven to go down to earth and live there; and being with God.

Memories came back to me. It was exciting. It gave me a calming reassurance that I was going to the place I was supposed to go, and this was all part of the bigger picture.

I got to a point where I finished my ascension vertically—along with others near me. My spirit stopped for just a second. Then, I floated horizontally. Again, it happened naturally, without me doing anything.

As I floated forward, I noticed all of us spirits heading toward a landing area. We could see it from a distance and were admiring it as we got closer.

This landing station was like a huge receiving station with spirits floating above a platform. The platform was long—maybe a hundred miles long. I could not see the beginning or end of it. It was simple in design but adorned with gold all along it. It sparkled and shined like it was recently polished. The platform was maybe 40 or 50 yards deep, and beyond that, it looked like a beautiful park with trees, green grass, and thousands of flowers. It was stunning.

I studied the platform, as I floated closer to it. Somehow, I knew that I would stop floating when I reached the platform. This was Heaven's gate. It was warm and bright, with white puffy clouds, a blue sky, and a lot of spirits. Billions of spirits.

I watched as spirits that were in front of me landed on the platform and were greeted by other spirits. Family members. Lots of family members—like possibly every generation since the beginning of time. I guess that was God's way of welcoming spirits back home to Him—with family members they knew on earth and relatives who lived decades before them.

Spirits were everywhere—floating, meeting, cheering, and coaching others. But as I got closer, I could tell they were all younger, like 20- and 30-year-olds. I wondered what happened to older people. Why were only the younger spirits allowed to welcome people who died?

I could tell that each spirit took on the basic looks of the person's body it resided in. Spirits were not scary, like a ghost. Although I realized that's what they were. Spirits looked like a person with a face, body, arms, and legs that were glowing white.

All the spirits I could see wore long white robes that also glowed constantly. They looked happy. There was no way anyone could've been scared with so much happiness and such a warm, loving feeling.

Many spirits hovered around the receiving area where I was headed. My spirit floated right to my position on the receiving platform naturally. And there as I landed, I was greeted by several younger people I didn't recognize.

"Jake," a 30-something guy yelled out at me.

"Do I know you?"

"Jake, it's grandpa."

"And grandma," she said.

"What? How?"

They sounded like my grandparents but looked much younger.

"It's us. We have spirit bodies of our younger selves," grandpa said.

"Grandma and grandpa!" I shouted in excitement when I realized it was really them.

"My dear Jake," grandma said.

When I realized it was them, I was so excited that I lunged toward them. I tried to hug them, but I couldn't. I floated right through them. Without a body, spirits can't hug each other.

They laughed.

"That happens all the time," grandpa said.

I was amazed that I could float through another person's spirit. My mind inspected my spirit body further to see how it worked. I was in awe of the ability I had to float through solid objects, bodies, buildings, and other spirits.

"Welcome home," grandma said. "We're so glad to see you."

"Home? I can't believe I'm here," I said, still in shock over the whole thing, and trying unsuccessfully to hug them again.

Grandpa laughed again at my failed attempt to hug him. "As a spirit, you have all the mental and emotional characteristics that you had on earth. But you can't do anything physical."

"Like hugging," I said, still amazed at where I was and the spiritual condition I was in.

"We can't hug, but there is a special way spirits show love," grandma said.

Grandma looked good: young and full of life. That was ironic since she was dead. Her long hair glowed, and while she always had the biggest smile on her face on earth, it seemed even bigger here.

"Put your hand against mine," she said.

I raised my right hand and held it chest high. She slowly put her hand up to mine. She placed her spirit palm up to mine. I couldn't feel it, but I could see that our palms were right next to each other. Then, she made sure her fingers lined up against mine, one by one.

As soon as that connection was completely made, our hands warmed up and glowed brighter. While I couldn't feel temperature, my spirit felt a warmth of love from the connection we made. The glow of our hands "touching" was brighter than they were normally, and even had a red glow to it. The feeling consumed me with love for my grandparents.

Oh, how I had missed them. Their death had been hard for our whole family. And now, I got to be with them again. That made me realize the difficulty my family was feeling over my tragic death back on earth... and wonder when I would see them again.

"We are so excited to see you here," said grandpa, putting his hand up for me to connect with him.

Grandpa and I had a special bond. I could tell him anything. He always loved me no matter what I did. Having them greet me made me feel so much better to be here. And connecting our hands let him know that.

"We love you so much!" grandpa said.

My grandpa, Rex Peterson, was a cool guy. Grandpa was a college football player and still looked the part. He was tall, well-built and had a face like a movie star. Grandma Cathy was his high school sweetheart, and together they were the perfect couple. Grandma Cathy was the nicest person who was always loving to everyone.

"We are assigned to be your hosts," grandma said.

There was so much I wanted to know about being a spirit after dying. What do we do here? How long are we here? Can I visit my family and friends and Katie back on earth? Can I send them a message? Do I have any way to communicate with people back on earth?

"What does a host do?" I asked. "And what do spirits do?"

"Hosts get to be your guide through this part of your journey," grandpa said.

"My journey?"

"Yes," said grandpa. "This is all part of the plan and here in heaven, we help people on earth."

"Spirits do God's work on earth," grandma said. "We get assignments, and we visit people on earth and help influence them to do good."

"We are God's messengers," grandpa said. "We fight against evil."

"I thought heaven was floating on clouds all day and playing harps," I joked.

"Not here." He laughed. "There is a lot of work to do," he said seriously.

"So, I can go back to earth?" I asked hopefully.

"At some point you will. But first, you need to meet all your relatives," grandpa said pointing toward a large group of people. "These are my parents, your great-grandparents Dan and Kim Peterson."

"Jake it's so great to see you again," great-grandpa Dan said.

"Again?" I said confused.

"Yes, you were here before you were born," Kim said. "We spent time together getting you ready to go to earth before you were born."

"And these are my parents," grandma said, "your other great-grandparents, Tom and Carrie Thatcher."

"Great to meet you," I said, still surprised that they all looked so young.

"Oh Jake," Carrie said, "we were also here with you in Heaven before you were born too."

"Sure," I said, trying to be polite.

"It's ok. It takes a little while for everything to come back to you," Tom said. "But in time, you'll remember everything about life before earth."

"Great."

Then grandpa introduced me to my great-grandparents on my mom's side, and then going back further—introducing me to generations of my family on both my mother's and father's side. It was exciting. I felt so much love there.

As I met each one, I was amazed at the amount of love and joy I felt from each of them. They knew me, and they loved me regardless of my weaknesses. It was amazing.

Each of my relatives had the bright glow that all spirits have here. And each was so happy and young-looking. Their faces literally shined with brightness, love, and the feeling of true happiness. I wondered how and why they were so happy here – after all, they were dead.

But something about their countenance told me that this was a place where all my troubles and stress of earth life would be gone. I felt it was the place I was supposed to be—part of the master plan, like grandpa said. And just knowing I was in the right place brought me peace.

As I met each of them, I put my hand up to each of their hands to show family love. The warmth I felt from each of them was overpowering. I felt so alive and happy. And yet, I was still dead.

I wanted to tell them about my family and what was going on with each of us, but they already knew.

"Each of us has been involved in your life since we got here," grandpa said. "We never really left you—only physically."

That surprised me. "What do you mean?"

"We get to make visits to earth to check on family from time to time," grandpa said. "We also get special requests to make visits to have a positive influence on the lives of our family members."

I thought I had felt the presence of my grandparents a few times after they died and now, I knew why.

I was excited that I was going to be able to see my family and Katie again. "Can I go down and visit right now?"

"Not yet," grandma said. "We have to give you an orientation first."

"Orientation?"

"Every new arrival has to have an orientation. It's part of the process," said grandpa.

"Come with us," grandma said. We waved to all the generations of family that I met and floated out of the receiving area to get a tour of heaven.

Together we floated around Heaven as they showed me everything. It's absolutely perfect. Picture the most beautiful scenery you've seen on earth, and then multiply it by a million. It's spectacular: light, warm, kind, and such a feeling of love and acceptance. It's vastly different than the destruction, crime, anger, and hatred that I experienced on earth.

Most of heaven was a wide-open area, with fields, flowers, and trees. I had never seen so many flowers. Each was colorful and pristine. Reds and blues and yellows and purples and oranges, in more vibrant colors than you could ever imagine. Trees and bushes were everywhere, giving it the sense of earth, but these were different. Greener and pristine. Trees seem to serve the purpose of providing happiness since their oxygen production has no value in heaven. There were no dead flowers, dead branches, dead leaves, and no weeds. It was absolutely amazing!

Everything looked stunning and impeccable and glowed. There were many buildings that are symmetrical and immaculate. I wondered what the buildings were needed for. Did they have business meetings in heaven?

There were animals: many colorful birds, bugs, mammals, and more. Every living creature in Heaven seemed to live in harmony. You could sense it. As I was taking it all in, I realized Heaven is beyond comparison to anything we have on earth.

Everything about Heaven was perfect. There is impeccable order in this place, and it was so beautiful. It is interesting that everyone is equal. There are no social classes, no racial inequality, no political parties, no winners, and no losers. No sackcloths and no EDM's. And everyone was happy.

As we toured, I was greeted by almost every spirit I passed. Every spirit was friendly; offering a simple "hello" or having a brief conversation to find out that we knew some of the same people.

Spirits are remarkable. Without a body, no one feels any pain. You still have your thoughts and emotions, though, and you glow with light.

As my grandparents took me around heaven, they taught me many things about pre-earth life, death, and post-earth life. They reminded me of the importance of choosing good over evil and said they were proud of my actions on earth. They taught me about the plan of eternal salvation, and that we were going to help teach the spirits of deceased people who never heard of Jesus Christ. That was another one of our responsibilities as spirits.

"Heavenly Father and Jesus visit us occasionally, but they will live here with us constantly after the Second Coming," grandpa said.

"I was wondering," I said.

"Yes, that will be a glorious time when we have them here with us permanently," he said.

The spirits were divided into two groups: spirits that have already lived on earth and are now deceased, and those who are still waiting to go to earth—to be spirits in bodies of newborn babies. Every spirit is happy. And every spirit helps each other. This is a place where we serve others, making it a very happy place.

We went by the area of spirits who were going to be born on earth soon—the birthing departure area. They were in small groups, being trained about what to do when they got there—which I thought was funny because once you are born on earth, no one remembers anything about living in Heaven or whatever training we got before being born.

Grandpa could sense my lack of understanding.

"We're programmed to forget life before earth. New spirits are taught eternal truths before they are born so that when they learn them on earth, their spirit will be more likely to remember," grandpa said. "It's critical for all new spirits to get that training."

As we floated around this platform of spirits ready to go down to earth, I noticed a male spirit hovering by himself.

Grandpa noticed I was looking at this spirit and said, "Come on, let's go meet him."

"Sure," I said.

"Do you have your departure plans yet?" grandpa asked him.

"Oh, I'm not leaving," he said. "I had my chance."

"What do you mean you had your chance?" I asked.

"I was aborted," said the man. "So, I never got to really experience life with a body."

"You don't get another chance to go back and grow up on earth?" I asked.

"No. It's fine. It's all part of the master plan that some spirits aren't going to spend any time on earth."

"My name is Rex Peterson; this is my wife Cathy, and this is my grandson Jake," grandpa said.

"Nice to meet you all," the spirit said.

"What's your name?" I asked.

"Chandler," he said.

"No way! My best friend on earth was a Chandler too," I said.

"He must have been really cool," Chandler joked.

Spirit Chandler looked cool for a spirit—like someone I'd hang out with if he went to my high school. He looked like the type of guy that had your back and that you could joke around with. But I quickly found out he had a serious side to him too.

"I ask every new spirit I meet, what's it like living down there?" he said.

"On earth?"

"Yes. What's it like? I've been able to visit people when called to serve others down there, but I know that's not the same as having a body and actually living there."

"I want to know what it feels like to play sports, to go to school and to have a girlfriend," spirit Chandler said.

"Oh wow," I said, taken back by his question. "It's amazing. Having a body is cool. You can run, jump, catch and do all kinds of things. I played football, so I got to hit people on the field."

"Hitting people is fun?" spirit Chandler joked.

"Well, in that situation it is. But there's a lot more you can do. I liked running, riding bikes, lifting weights too."

"So how did it feel to be able to run? Is it better than floating?"

I could tell he felt a little cheated out of life on earth. "It's great fun, but floating is exciting too. I'm blown away by the ability we have to float through things and float so quickly. I could never run that fast."

"I have days where I wish I had another chance," Chandler said contemplating his situation. "But I'm totally happy being here."

"I'm sorry you didn't get the chance."

"No worries. I just like hearing what it's like."

"Definitely understand."

"Hey, I'm going to call you 'spirit Chandler' if that's ok."

"Sure. And let me know if you ever need someone to join you on an assignment to earth. Maybe you could show me around where you lived and the things you did."

"That sounds great."

"Well Jake," grandpa said. "We need to go."

"Come see me any time," spirit Chandler said.

"All right spirit Chandler, we've gotta run… or I guess fly," I said.

He laughed while my grandparents and me floated away from the birthing departure area.

I wanted to stay longer to talk with my new spirit friend, but I knew we'd see him again.

We floated back into the receiving area where spirits who had died were now coming back.

"There are a lot more spirits here in the receiving area than in the birthing area," I said.

"Yes," grandma said. "It used to be the other way around—a few decades ago, there were more spirits ready to go to earth. But now, we're nearing the end of new spirits ready to be born."

"Jake, we are getting close to the time of the Second Coming of Jesus Christ," grandpa said. "Seeing the dwindling number of new birth departures is a sure sign that the end is near."

"What's going to happen then?" I asked. "When all the spirits are gone to earth?"

"I don't know for sure," grandpa said. "But I know we just keep doing the things we're doing."

"What things are you doing?"

"For starters, we are being a positive influence on family members on earth so they make the best decisions. That's been our most important job since we got here. The spirits with earth experience can be a positive influence on family members there since they've lived there already."

"One thing I know about the end is that all spirits are going to lead the way for the Second Coming by floating down to earth in an enormous circle of angels and singing to announce His arrival."

"When is the Second Coming?" I asked.

"No one knows," said grandma. "But we've been practicing for our part for some time."

"Like choir?" I said.

"I guess so," grandma replied.

"Do they need any help?" I asked.

"Yes. You'll have a part in it too," said grandma. "Every spirit does."

"They'll have another practice soon, and you'll get to participate," said grandpa. "It's so fun!"

"What do we practice?" I asked.

"You'll see," they said. "Now we need to give you some of the rules of being here," grandpa said.

As we floated around, my grandparents told me about the condition spirits are in. We can freely go anywhere but are to abide by standard rules of conduct, which included that we stay in Heaven, unless we're on an assignment.

Assignments are given regularly. Those assigned go to earth for a specific mission. They are to complete the mission and then return. It's ok to stop in on family after the mission is completed but not for long periods of time. Spirits are not visible to people on earth. That way, we can be messengers on earth without being seen.

Spirits are not allowed to be present at inappropriate times, such as when humans are dressing/undressing, going to the bathroom, showering, being intimate, and that sort of thing. It's rules that protect the privacy of humans and keeps our spirit minds pure and capable of helping anyone at any time.

CHAPTER 17

KATIE'S SHOCK

Back on earth, Katie arrived home and was excited to get upstairs to her room and read the card I left her.

She parked at her house and let her friends out there since they all lived in her cul-de-sac. She handed out each of their bags from her trunk hurriedly and said quick goodbyes. Then, she grabbed her bags and ran inside.

"Welcome home Katie, how was the trip?" her mother asked, as she came through the door.

"It was great. Thank you so much for letting me go," she said rushing up the stairs toward her bedroom.

"Tell us all about it dear," her mom said.

"I will, but I'd really like to read the card from Jake first. Is that ok?" She hurried up the stairs to her room.

"Of course," her dad said.

She paused halfway up the stairs, turned around and said, "Oh, dad… can you please call the sheriff's office and let them know that I hit a deer on the Connector?"

"You went on the Connector tonight?" her mother asked.

"You hit another deer?" her father asked.

"Yes, I think it was a small one because the bump was not as much as the last time. We saw a lot of deer in the field and Susan was shining a flashlight out there to see their eyes. We must have spooked one who ran onto the road."

"Are you ok? Any damage to the Hummer?" her dad asked.

"I'm fine and I'm sure the car is fine too," she said. "I barely felt anything."

"OK, I'll call the police and report it. Then let's hear more about the trip."

While Katie took her bags up to her room, her dad went to the driveway to inspect Katie's SUV. With a flashlight, Katie's dad saw a broken turn signal light, a dent in the front driver's side of the hood, some blood on the grill, as well as a black mark—which came from my helmet. While he wasn't sure how a deer left a black mark, he thought the blood was from the deer and quickly called the sheriff's office to report it.

He called while outside observing the damage. The sheriff's office thanked him and said they'd send two deputies to remove the deer from the road right away and make it safe for anyone that might be traveling down the road.

"Is there much damage to her car?" Katie's mom asked when he returned to the house.

"Not too bad. We'll need a new turn signal light, a small dent repair and maybe a little touch-up paint. But it's a good thing we bought her a Hummer. That deer got the worst of it, I'm sure," her dad said. "I'll get her car washed and detailed tomorrow and then we'll assess the damage further. I'm just glad she's ok."

Just then, Katie let out a loud scream from her room. "NO!" she cried. "Oh no, no, no!!"

Her mom and dad rushed up to her room to see what caused such an outburst.

Katie wept uncontrollably. My letter was on the floor. She thought the message was going to be different.

Katie's mom picked up the card and read it:

My Katie,

This has been the hardest decision of my life. You know my standards. Those standards are what bring me so much happiness. But you bring me so much happiness too. You've asked me to choose between following God my way or following you. Since the day you asked me to make my decision, I've struggled with the question greatly. I've felt that you and I have the potential for a great future together, but you know I don't believe in breaking the rules. So, as hard as this is to say, my decision is to love you forever but not as your boyfriend. I have chosen to follow the path that I feel is right, not your path. I will always love you and will always wonder what could have happened between us, but sadly, I must let you go.

All my love,

Jake

Katie sat on the bed and sobbed. Her mom hugged her and tried to calm her down, but she was inconsolable.

"I am so sorry Katie," she said as she hugged her close. They sat there for a long time. Katie had never cried that much. She had expected that I would change for her.

"Oh mom," she said. "I love him so much."

"I know, I know," she said as she held Katie close.

Responding to her dad's phone call, two police officers went to the Connector to search for a dead deer. They turned on their emergency lights to slow down any traffic that might be on the road. But there was no one on the Connector. They began searching along the road for the deer but found nothing.

They saw deep tire tracks in the gravel and thought that was the place where Katie hit the deer, so they stopped and one of the officers got out and looked over the edge.

The officer called to his partner who came over to help.

"That's no deer," he said looking at my body.

"No," said the officer who found me. He was a new officer who had never seen a dead body. The shock of my dead, bloody, mangled body made him vomit.

They called in another squad car as well as the coroner to get my body and examine it. The two additional officers arrived quickly, and they searched the entire ditch along the road to see if there were any other recent deer carcasses. Perhaps I was killed days ago, and there was also a deer killed tonight, they thought.

However, after an exhaustive search they found no dead deer in the ditch, the fields or on the road.

Realizing they had a vehicular homicide on their hands, they called the sheriff. While the officers searched my body for ID and looked around it for evidence, the sheriff immediately drove to the Martin's home.

Walking up to the door, the sheriff noticed Katie's Hummer. Shining his flashlight, he saw blood and hair on her SUV. My blood and my hair. He took a sample.

It was only 10:45 but Katie had fallen asleep, emotionally exhausted. The sheriff knocked on the door and Katie's dad answered.

"Sorry to bother you so late," the sheriff said.

"Oh, hi Sheriff. No worries. We're still up. Did you find that deer?"

"No, but may I come in?"

"Of course. What's going on?"

The sheriff sat down and let out a big sigh.

"My men looked all over the Connector and didn't find a deer."

"No? Are you sure?"

"Yes, I'm sure. No deer," said the sheriff.

"So, what did Katie hit?" her dad asked.

"They found a body of a boy hit by a car."

"NO!" said Katie's dad. "Who is it and how did it happen?"

"Is your daughter home?" said the sheriff.

"Yes, but–"

"I need to speak to her," the sheriff interrupted.

"She hit a deer, not a boy," her dad said, with worry in his voice.

"Isn't she 18?" asked the officer.

"Yes" said her dad. "But what does she have to do with this boy?"

"Then I can speak with her directly. You can be present."

At that point, Katie's mom had come to the living room, and she could sense something bad was about to happen.

Katie's dad went upstairs and woke her up. He asked her if she saw the deer she hit.

"No," she said in a groggy voice. "It happened fast and I was looking into the field when I hit it. Why?"

"Because the sheriff is here and wants to talk to you."

"Dad, I had a little to drink tonight on the way home," she said with tears running down her face.

"Oh Katie, this doesn't look good," he said, hugging her immediately and sensing what was about to happen.

She slowly walked downstairs and saw the sheriff in her living room. "What's going on?" she asked hesitantly, her face a mess of makeup from crying so much.

"Your dad called my office a few hours ago and said you hit a deer on the Connector," the sheriff said.

"Yes, but that's not against the law, is it?" she said. "It was an accident."

"No—hitting a deer is not against the law," he said. "Did you actually see the deer you hit? Did you stop and look at it?"

"Well, no. I didn't see it, I just felt it. And we drove on because we had to get home."

"My officers searched the road, the ditch and the fields and didn't find any deer."

"Are you sure?" she said. "Then what did I hit?"

"Officers found the body of a dead boy on a bike in the ditch."

"No!" said Katie and her mom, almost in unison.

"Who is it?" her dad asked.

"We don't know yet," the sheriff said. "He had no ID on him. We're still looking into it. Given the fact that you admitted you hit something, and there was no deer on the road, and judging by the blood and hair on your car, it's very possible that you killed this boy with your vehicle

"NO!" Katie screamed. "There's no way," she said in unbelief. "I would have known if I hit a person."

She was sitting close enough to the sheriff that he smelled the alcohol on her breath.

"Katie, were you driving drunk tonight?"

She was not able to speak. She knew she made a big mistake. She knew she hit *something*.

"You might want to call your lawyer," the sheriff said to her father. "I need to go to my vehicle for a couple minutes while you have that conversation. I'll be back."

At the car, the sheriff called a judge to get a warrant for Katie's arrest. It only took a few minutes for the judge to email it to him, and he was back at the door. Katie's father let him in.

The sheriff took out his handcuffs and said "I have a warrant for your arrest. Katie Martin, you are under arrest for driving while intoxicated and the possible vehicular manslaughter of the deceased boy, pending investigation."

"No!" Katie cried.

"Wait! You can't do this," her dad said. "Do you even have enough evidence to take her?"

"Yes, we do." He read her rights to her and said, "Come with me," as he walked her out the front door.

"Can we meet you at the station?" her mother said.

"You can come down there, but she's going to have to spend the night in jail and you can post bail in the morning," he said.

Katie was sobbing, somewhat disoriented and shocked by what was happening.

The sheriff stopped outside his car and gave her a breathalyzer test.

"Point zero five," he said. "Not good."

Katie burst into tears again as she sat in the back of the police car.

Her parents got in their car and headed to the police station behind the sheriff. They wondered what they would do at the station if they couldn't take her home tonight. But they decided to go and support their daughter any way they could.

My body was picked up by the coroner. I had no ID on me—who carries a wallet when riding a bike? So, I was a John Doe for a while. The officers found my cell phone in the ditch and ran a search for my address based on my cell phone number. They found out within a few minutes who I was.

"He was Jake Peterson," said one of the officers.

"The football player?" asked the other.

"Yes, the football player," he said, shaking his head in disbelief.

"No way!"

Across town, my parents had been wondering what happened to me and were growing more worried. They had a sick feeling inside before the officers even got there. Sometimes parents just know things. Mine were especially in tune.

The officers showed up at my home around midnight and knocked gently on the door. It took a few minutes for my parents to answer the door.

"Mr. and Mrs. Peterson?" the officers asked.

"Yes," said my dad. "What's this about?"

"Can we come in please?"

"Yes, what's going on?" my dad asked.

Stepping into the living room and sitting down, the officers said, "This is about your son Jake."

"Is he okay? He should be home soon."

"Mr. and Mrs. Peterson, we found Jake's body on the side of the Connector. He was hit by a car and has passed away."

"Oh no," my mom cried.

"No!" my dad said in shock, putting his face in his hands.

Minutes passed while my parents grieved quietly.

"I know this is hard to take, but we need you to come to the coroner's office in the morning and identify the body," one of the officers said.

The officers told them what they knew about the situation, which wasn't much. They said that I likely did not suffer much, that the impact probably killed me instantly. But that gave my parents only a little comfort.

My parents had many questions: Who did it? Why was I on the Connector? Who would leave after hitting me?

My parents sobbed. They were shocked.

"We have started an investigation into the accident," said one of the officers. "We have a couple of leads already, and hopefully we will bring justice to your family very soon. We are so sorry for your loss."

As my parents hugged each other, the officers excused themselves and headed for the door.

"Thank you for telling us," my dad said through his tears as he got up to let them out.

"I'm so sorry," the officer said. "I can't imagine the pain that you must feel," he said.

After the police officers left, my parents woke Jane and Zack and told them of the tragedy. It was a very sad night for them. A really long night for my family. Very few words were said, but sometimes you don't need words to communicate.

My family got no sleep. My parents called other relatives around 1:00 in the morning to tell them the news. My Aunt Nancy volunteered to take my brother and sister the next day so my parents could go to the coroner's office. She and Uncle Ray lived close and could easily pick them up and take them for the entire day.

In the morning, exhausted from the emotions of my death and so little sleep, my parents went to see the coroner at eight a.m. when the office opened.

As they walked up the sidewalk to the front door, my parents were still stunned and in a daze. The coroner's office was a basic office building with nothing special about the design. There was a small waiting area in the lobby with three chairs and a receptionist who didn't have the most pleasant job.

"We are here to identify the body of Jake Peterson," my father said to the receptionist, while his voice cracked.

"The boy who was killed on the Connector," the coroner's receptionist said. "Very sad."

My mom couldn't speak. She was crying again.

The receptionist called the coroner who came to the front desk almost immediately. She had been waiting for my parents. The coroner was a middle-aged woman who looked very professional. Her white lab coat had dabs of blood on it in a few spots that looked fresh. My mom noticed the blood on her lab coat and wondered if it was my blood.

"Follow me," said the coroner quietly. "We think he died instantly," she said, leading my parents into the room where they kept the bodies.

The morgue is an eerie place. Just knowing it's a hotel for dead bodies to stay until their funerals is weird enough, but it also smells bad, like a frog dissection experiment gone wrong.

The coroner walked to the tray where my body was. Each tray was made of shiny stainless steel with a big handle. I was in tray 12 on the bottom. She pulled out my tray, and then paused and said, "He took a major blow to the head from the on-coming car. It crushed his skull into his brain, and that killed him instantly. Please be aware that the collision disfigured his head and face, so he may not be instantly recognizable to you. I need you to be prepared for what you are about to see."

"OK," my dad said, not sure if he even wanted to see my body. My mom was crying again as the coroner pulled my tray out. My body was covered with a sheet that was white, except for some blood stains around my head and chest. The coroner pulled the sheet back just far enough to see my face.

My mom knew that it was me and instantly started sobbing.

"He felt nothing," said the coroner again. She gave my parents a minute.

They both stood there looking at my face, in shock, saying nothing, while tears streamed down their faces.

The coroner could sense that my parents needed some time alone, so she walked to the door.

"I need to be present when you confirm that this is your son," she said, holding the door open. "Afterward, if you'd like to spend a little time alone with the body, you can do that."

I had a birthmark on my right shoulder that my mom recognized. They also looked at my eyes and teeth…what was left of them.

"It's him," my mother said, fighting back more tears.

"Yes, it is," dad said.

"OK. I'll give you a few minutes," said the coroner. She walked out closing the door and both of my parents broke down again.

CHAPTER 18

KATIE'S HELL/MY HEAVEN

K atie's jail cell was four walls of solid concrete and a small steel door that looked like it could withstand a thousand bullets. There was a small cot in the corner with a lumpy mattress and a toilet with no privacy. The entire situation was surreal, and it was about to get worse.

The evidence against Katie was easy to get. The hair and blood samples on her car were just the beginning. There was also a fragment of paint from her car lodged into my bike helmet and another one found in my forehead. The fact that she knew she hit something hard enough to ask her dad to call the sheriff was further proof. Driving drunk was another piece of damning evidence.

She was guilty, and she knew it.

She had spent the night in jail and was waiting for her parents to post bail that morning.

During this whole ordeal, Katie had been focusing on what was going to happen to her next. She was worried about spending years in jail and how that would forever change her life… until she had a visitor to her jail cell.

As soon as my parents confirmed that it was my body on the tray, the coroner's office published that I was the deceased person. Everyone in the sheriff's office saw it. The sheriff realized that I was the same age as Katie, and that we went to the same high school. So he decided to tell Katie while she was in her cell.

As he walked toward her cell, his heart felt heavy for the pain he knew Katie was going through, and for what would happen to her if she was found guilty.

"Katie, the identity of the deceased boy was announced this morning," he said. "And I think you may know him—he went to your school."

"Oh no. Who?" she said, fighting the tears.

"His name was Jake Peterson."

"OH NO!" she cried. She sobbed uncontrollably. "No, no, no," she kept saying.

"You knew him?" the sheriff asked.

Katie couldn't answer through the tears and the pain that rushed through her entire body. She fell to the ground. Not only were we broken up, but she was the cause of my death. The emotional trauma was more than Katie could handle.

The sheriff left her jail cell, and Katie was still sobbing when her parents came 30 minutes later. They were present for the booking the night before, but quickly realized there was nothing they could do until morning. Visiting hours started at 9:30 AM and they were there at 9:30 sharp.

"We are here to see Katie Martin," Jeff said at the front desk of the sheriff's office, still shaken up by the whole ordeal.

"What relationship are you to Ms. Martin?" asked the clerk with a little attitude.

"We are her parents," Jeff said.

Her parents were very anxious to see Katie and hoped to find a way out for her. But the clerk seemed to take forever to produce the paperwork they needed to sign, and Jeff was frustrated.

"OK, I need some ID from both of you. Then read and sign this," she said. "And this." She slid another form in front of them.

"What do these mean?" her dad asked.

"You can read them," said the clerk, who wasn't in the mood to explain things. She knew that Katie killed me, and she was angry at the Martins because of it.

"No bail amount has been set for her release yet," said the clerk.

"Why not?" Jeff asked. "The sheriff said we could post bail this morning."

"Sometimes the judge takes longer to decide on bail, especially in a murder case like this," said the clerk.

"It's not murder," Hannah whispered.

"As soon as the judge makes the decision, you will be notified," the clerk responded.

An officer came to take them to the visitation room. She was a mean-looking officer who was taller than most people. With short red hair and biceps that were bigger than most of the guys on my football team, I doubt anyone would mess with her.

She took them to a room with thick glass walls where family members were permitted to visit with inmates. The pale white walls and beat-up chairs were like something out of a bad movie. After all, why would the jail want to make people feel comfortable! It was cold and unwelcoming and not the kind of place where anyone wanted to hang out.

Katie was brought to the visiting room by two guards. Her face red from tears, her eyes looked like she hadn't slept in a month, and her freshly pressed orange jump suit looked extra big on her small body. She was exhausted. When she saw her parents, it was the first good thing she'd experienced in hours.

"Oh Katie," her mom said, as she picked up the phone on the other side of the glass.

"Mom, it was Jake," she said with the tears flowing again.

"What do you mean? What happened to Jake?" Hannah asked, confused by Katie's comment.

"It was Jake on the bike on the Connector. I hit Jake with my car. I killed Jake!" she said sobbing.

"Oh no," Jeff said, feeling like he'd just lost his own son. He looked up and saw a camera in the corner of the room with a blinking red light.

Her parents couldn't believe it. Katie's life would change forever. They had such great hopes and dreams for her. This was their little girl. She was supposed to live a great life. Now due to her actions, her life would change forever.

The evidence against her was too great, and Katie's "future" was likely going to be limited to that oversized orange jump suit in a 6x6 cell at the state pen.

The situation grieved Katie's parents so much. They wanted to hug her but couldn't. They wanted to assure her that everything would be ok, but it wouldn't. They tried to console her but couldn't.

The fact that the judge was not setting a bail amount yet made the morning more challenging for the Martins. That was hard for Katie to take, after expecting to leave with her parents that morning.

After their allotted 15-minute visit, Katie was taken from the visiting area by two guards who showed no compassion for her. Sobbing as she was taken away, the pain was nearly too much for her parents as well.

The news spread quickly around town through social media. Within a few hours, everyone knew that I died, and that the person that killed me was Katie. The whole town was in shock over it. Kids from school were so sad. That day, many people made signs with my jersey #50 on it and put them in the windows of their homes and businesses as a tribute to me. That was such an honor, but at that point, I was more concerned about Katie.

My dad got a call from the sheriff's office with an update on the case. He was told that Katie was the suspect, that she was driving under the influence and that she had admitted killing me on cameras in the jail's visiting area. Dad was shocked, as he hung up the phone.

The look on his face told my mom that he just got more devastating news.

"What now?" she asked, not ready for any more bad news.

"That was the sheriff's office" he said slowly and in disbelief. "They have a suspect already."

"Who is it?" she asked, not sure if she really wanted to know.

"It's…it's…" my dad was in such shock he could hardly speak. "It's Katie."

"Jake's Katie?"

"Yes. But it was an accident. She didn't even know."

"Oh no. Poor Katie," my mom said through more tears. "Could this get any worse?"

"They said she admitted to hitting something but thought it was a deer. They also said she was driving intoxicated."

"Intoxicated? Katie? Oh no," mom said in disbelief.

My parents were very forgiving people—even to someone who killed their son. They knew that being angry at Katie or her family was not going to bring me back. And they said a prayer asking God to help them forgive, and to give Katie the strength she would need for this difficult challenge ahead of her.

You might think someone that can forgive that easily is a push over. But my parents had a very realistic view on life, and they knew the bigger plan for life after death—that it was our goal to live good enough lives so we could live with God again someday. And while they might have some feelings of anger toward Katie, they knew they must forgive her and love her, as hard as that would be for any parent who loses a child.

My family quickly became overwhelmed with an out-pouring of love from members of our church and community. Many people stopped by randomly throughout the morning to drop off flowers and cards, bring food or to just give my family a hug.

Friends offered to help in any and every way possible. The love from everyone helped my family to deal with the pain of my death.

Many of my friends came to my parent's house to show support. Ben, Chandler, and Tyson stayed for hours. They finished off the food brought by friends. Eating is way to get comfort in times of pain, especially for my friends.

After a few hours, Katie's friends Susan, Sarah and Kellie came over. At first, my friends were uncomfortable with them being there, but when my mom welcomed them with a hug, they realized it was ok. Susan told my parents she was so sorry for what happened. The girls said they had made a commitment to never drink and drive again. My parents embraced them.

Usually, people know when they messed up. Susan, Sarah, and Kellie knew it. If my parents got upset with them and preached to them about drinking and driving, they would have left and never came back. But my parents showed love. They knew the girls had already been suffering during this whole ordeal and my parents took the high road—thinking that love might be the only way to get them to change. They were right.

Everyone sat and talked, which quickly evolved into a discussion about the great times we all had in high school. As they reminisced about our times together, it almost made them forget about the tragedy that happened.

Together, my friends planned a candlelight tribute for me at the football field the following night at eight PM. They asked the principal to conduct the assembly and she agreed. They also got coach Davidson and Ms. Parker to speak.

My parents asked everyone to leave the house around three o'clock so they could go to the funeral home to plan the funeral.

CHAPTER 19

MY FIRST ASSIGNMENT

Back in heaven, after my orientation, I got my first assignment. My grandparents and I were floating around the receiving area for the newly deceased when a tall messenger angel floated up to me. She was taller than most of the other spirit women and most women I saw on earth. Her long hair flowed like she was flying at high speeds, yet she was gliding gracefully toward me in her glowing white robe. Her eyes focused on me as she floated toward me. But what I noticed most was her smile. She looked so happy.

"Jake, my name is Angela," she said. "I'm here to give you your first assignment."

"Awesome," I said. "What do you need me to do?"

"We need you to support your parents, as they go to the funeral home to make your arrangements."

"Yes! I get to see my parents. That's great. When do I leave?"

"Jake, you need to know that this will not be a happy visit. Your parents are so sad for your loss. They need comfort. Your mission is to help them feel your presence and let them know you're ok here in heaven."

"But how am I supposed to do that?" I asked.

"You speak it and feel it in your heart. All you can do is deliver the message. It's up to them to hear it," she said.

"Jake, think of it as if you were alive and present," grandma said. "You'd sit beside them and say, 'Don't worry Mom and Dad, I'm ok,' right? You'd say, 'I'm happy and everything is going to be all right.'"

"Yeah, I guess so," I said. "But what if they don't listen?"

"Most people don't listen," Angela said. "But some do. And that's our hope—that your parents will be in tune with your spirit so they know everything will be ok. Once they realize that, they will have the strength to get through life without you in it."

"OK, I'll do my best."

"That's all we ask," Angela said.

"But how do I get back to earth?"

"There's a descension process that your grandparents will show you. And they can go with you if you want."

"Yes, I want them to go with me. Definitely."

"That's fine," Angela said. "The missions you're sent on require you to report back to the assignment angel. This first mission is to send peace and comfort. Do your best and that's good enough. I'll be here when you get back."

"Thank you so much for letting me see my parents."

"You're welcome. Now you'd better get going, as your parents are already on their way to the funeral home."

"Bye Angela," grandma said.

"Jake, the descension process is easy," grandpa said, as we floated away. "There are small descension platforms all over heaven. You saw many of them on our tour earlier. You can leave from any platform you want... like that one." He pointed to a platform where someone had just left.

These platforms were like small stages. They were about 10 feet by 10 feet and looked like a gold tray with side rails floating in the clouds.

"There is a sentinel standing on the platform who will record your mission plans," grandpa said, as we floated closer.

The sentinel for this platform was a short, skinny guy who looked more friendly than formal. I had expected a sentinel to be more like an armed guard in camo with a machine gun turret, but he acted more like a concerned parent.

"Hello there. What's your assignment?" he asked politely.

"We are going to comfort Jake Peterson's parents at the funeral home," grandpa said.

"Ah yes. That's a great cause," said the sentinel. "Go with faith and do your best."

"Thank you," I said, now feeling extra good about this cause.

"Return with honor," the sentinel said as we floated off the platform.

That was easy, I thought.

"We're going to float really fast Jake," said grandpa. "But because you are in spirit form, you won't even notice."

We floated toward earth crazy fast, through the dark sky. The earth glowed like a beacon of light inviting us to it.

He was right. I couldn't tell how fast we were going. What normally may have turned my stomach upside down and in knots wasn't affecting me in any way at all. Probably because I had no stomach.

"Man, we're moving fast, Grandpa!"

Looking at earth, it was astounding. The blue seas, green and brown areas. The puffy clouds. And the glow it had. I remembered being mesmerized by it when I died and was floating up to heaven. That seemed like months ago...

"Isn't it stunning Jake?" grandma asked.

"Yes. Unbelievable!"

"It's one of the benefits of getting an earth assignment—you get to see the beauty of the whole earth."

As we descended, we saw other spirits descending in the distance for other assignments as well. It looked like a very well-run team of helpers who were eager to get to their assignment.

I wondered where each of them was headed and what their assignment was. But I was so excited that my assignment was to be with my parents. I missed being with them, but as Angela said—I really was happy and everything was ok.

As we got closer to my town, we slowed for our approach to the funeral home.

The funeral home was an old red brick building with white trim, white doors, and a black roof. It looked like it could have been an old schoolhouse back in the day.

"Ready to float through walls?" grandpa asked.

"He loves doing that," grandma said.

We floated right up to the funeral home and through the brick wall. It was mind-blowing to travel that fast and then right through a wall without any harm or injury.

"We'll hover in the lobby and wait for your parents," grandma said.

"OK," I agreed, as I thought about how quickly we went from heaven to earth and how crazy it was to float through a wall. Amazing, I thought.

The lobby had a similar dated look. It's stained honey oak chair rail on white walls looked like something out of a 70's movie. The floor had a carpet that may have been red when it was new but was now mostly black from dirt. The décor was simple, as you'd expect in a funeral home. Few pictures. Nothing special.

"Are you excited to see your parents?" grandma asked.

"I can't wait to see them," I said, floating around the lobby still amazed at how quickly we got there.

Only a minute later, the door opened and in walked my parents.

My mom looked so tired—like she had been running a marathon all week. Her eyes were red and nearly matched the red shirt she had on. Her face was flush as if she was getting sick. But I knew it was from the sadness of my death.

Dad didn't look much better. His head was down, and he was quiet, which usually meant he was deep in thought. His eyes were a bit red too.

Only a couple days had passed, but oh how I missed them. In spirit form I no longer had a heart, but I know that if I did, it would be beating strongly. My whole countenance was beaming with love for them.

"Welcome Mr. and Mrs. Peterson," said the funeral director who met them in the lobby. "We are so sorry for your loss."

"Thank you," my dad said quietly.

The funeral director was a younger man—surprisingly young for a funeral director. Normal looking—not creepy like you'd envision some funeral directors would be. He was very sensitive to the situation my parents were going through, having likely done this hundreds of times.

He wore a black suit that fit him very well—tailor made for him. It was a modern looking suit, which made me wonder how much funerals cost and how much he makes a year. His wavy brown hair looked like he didn't do anything to it—it just naturally fell in place. He seemed kind and caring and not very pushy.

"Let's sit in my office and plan the details," he said.

As they sat, we floated in the air around them. I was in awe of the experience to see my parents in such a different way. I felt the love they had for me. I also felt the pain and suffering my death had caused them. I'm not sure how that's possible, but I felt their emotional pain and it hurt.

The funeral director started with the business of planning my arrangements. "The items we want to cover today are Jake's casket, flowers, and program...

"Go on Jake," grandpa said. "Start now."

"Float around your parents and tell them you're ok," grandma said. "They need to know."

"Here are pictures of the best caskets we offer and their prices," the funeral director said to my parents.

As my parents flipped through a catalog of caskets, still in shock from this entire thing, I floated around them and looked at them with great love for all the sacrifices they'd been through on my behalf.

"Mom... Dad. I'm ok," I said kind of awkwardly. "Like this grandpa?"

"Yes, but keep going. Sometimes it takes a while for people to feel your spirit in the room."

"I'm ok. I'm in a good place," I said to them while floating around their heads.

I repeated that a few times while I encircled them.

My mom struggled to hold back tears. I floated around her and said that I was happy, and everything would be ok.

I couldn't tell if she was getting my message. And that made me sad. I thought of the many times my parents tried teaching me something and I didn't hear, or didn't want to hear, or just didn't listen. I realized why they got frustrated with me from time to time.

Her eyes swelled up with big tears and I couldn't handle the emotions. Without a body, I couldn't cry or hug them. That was so hard.

Caught up in my emotions, I floated right in front of her face and said, "I love you Mom! So much!" I nearly yelled it as a way of expressing my emotions to her.

Then her eyes and ears perked up, as if she heard me. "Wait," she said to the funeral director.

He paused for a moment.

"I feel like he's here," she said to my dad.

"Jake?" my dad asked.

"Yes," she said. "He's ok, and he's even happy," she said.

"Grandma and grandpa, she got my message!" I said with great excitement.

"Well done, boy," grandpa said.

"It's not uncommon to feel a connection to your deceased family members," the funeral director said.

"You've seen this before?" dad asked.

"Yes, of course. Take a minute to feel his presence," the funeral director said, as he was quiet for a bit.

I did it. Somehow, my message got to my mom. She couldn't hear me because my voice wasn't audible on earth. But she could sense it... feel it.

That made me so happy! I could communicate with my parents and others! That's great!

We watched as my mom and dad hugged and both were smiling through their tears. We could see it in their eyes that they knew I was ok. Somehow, that made it easier to know that I would need to leave them soon.

"Well Jake, you did it," grandma said.

"Yes. Thank you for the training," I said. "How long can we stay?"

"You accomplished the job we had to do, so we should go soon," grandpa said.

"But there's something else we should do before we leave," grandma said.

"What's that?" I asked.

"Jake, it's important that you see your body before we go back," grandma said.

"Oh yeah," I said. "I guess I forgot that my body is here."

"It may be alarming to see it. Are you sure you're ready?" grandpa asked.

"Yes, let's do it."

The three of us stayed close to each other as we floated down the hallway toward the room where my body laid. We floated right through the door.

My body was on a gurney under a sheet, with only my chest and head exposed.

I stared at my dead body. As I floated above it, it was surreal knowing that was me on the gurney.

The blood stains were cleaned up. The cuts on my face were patched up. But I still looked really bad.

"You look terrible," grandpa said trying to be funny.

"Rex! Don't say that," grandma said.

"It's ok," I said. "I can't believe it's me," in awe by the whole experience.

"It's your body, but it's not the complete you," grandma said.

"Your spirit is who you are, Jake," grandpa said. "Your body is just what housed your spirit on earth. Everything about who you are and what you do and the character you have is your spirit. That's the real you."

"Thanks," I said. "That helps. So, your body is kind of like a glove on your hand—the hand, or your spirit, lives on. The glove is like your body—it can't do anything without your hand in it."

"Great analogy," grandpa said.

"Yes, we may use that example with others," grandma said.

"Let's go back and report to Angela," grandpa said.

As much as I didn't want to leave my parents, I knew we needed to go back and report how we did. And I was happy that I got to see my parents and very grateful that I was able to deliver the message that I was safe and happy.

CHAPTER 20

CANDELIGHT VIGIL

While my parents were making funeral preparations, the radical sackcloths held a meeting and denounced Katie Martin as a sinner who needed to be punished—and her family too. They felt they had to act on this, so they made plans to threaten Katie's family as a way to make restitution for her grievous sin.

They were ruthless. They decided to send Katie hate mail in her jail cell every day for weeks, condemning her for her sin and telling her she was going to rot in hell for what she did. They also decided to protest outside the Martin home in two nights and to call Katie's friends "friends of a killer" every time they saw them. They wanted to make their presence felt and make everyone who was friends with Katie realize what a mistake she made by taking a life—even though it was an accident.

Somehow, they thought this was going to bring restitution for my death, or perhaps make Katie feel any worse than she already did. But the only way to resolve problems of this magnitude is with love.

The next night was the candlelight service on the football field. I got to go down to earth to be there. It was my second visit back, and my grandparents joined me.

It was an honor to see the work that went into that event, which was all planned in a few hours. The stadium was packed. Everyone from school was there... except Katie.

The stands were full of students, teachers, parents, and many people from the community. There was a sad, solemn feeling over the crowd. And everyone was mostly quiet out of shock and respect.

Everyone was given a candle when they entered the stadium. A simple white candle with a small paper plate near the bottom to catch the hot wax that fell.

On the field was a stage set up with eight chairs on it—filled by Principal Evans, Coach Davidson, Ms. Parker, Chandler, and my family.

Principal Evans conducted the ceremony and started promptly at eight, as planned.

"Students, friends and family, we want to welcome you here tonight to celebrate and honor the life of Jake Peterson. Jake was a model student who was loved by all. He was senior class president, the starting linebacker on the football team, and had a 4.0 GPA. He was a friend to everyone.

"For those who knew Jake, you know he was a good guy. He did many things right. He was kind and caring. And yet he was still a ferocious member of our football team."

A few people in the crowd let out a cheer after that.

"Jake was taken from us too early," she continued. "His death was such a shock to all of us. We're here tonight to remember him.

A candlelight vigil is a short ceremony to honor a person who dies tragically."

"So tonight, we've asked Jake's football coach, Mr. Jeff Davidson to say a few words. He will be followed by Ms. Debbie Parker, Jake's student government advisor. Then, one of Jake's many friends, Chandler Smith, will say a few words before leading us in the candlelight ceremony."

"At the conclusion of the candlelight vigil, we ask that all of you extinguish your candles and exit the stadium quietly, to show respect for Jake. Thank you all for attending and we remind you to be respectful this evening."

"Coach," she said, announcing him as the first speaker.

Coach Davidson was usually a fast walker and fast talker. He moved with energy. But that night, he took a lot of time to walk up to the microphone.

"Thank you, Principal Evans," coach said. Then, as he tried to start his speech, he couldn't. He wiped tears from his eyes. The crowd could see his struggle. As his voice cracked, he said "The news of Jake's death shocked me. Even now, after a few days, I really can't believe he's gone. Jake Peterson was invincible. He could do anything. He was strong and athletic, but he was also smart. He could control his emotions, so he played with great insight for the game. He's the reason our defense was so great last year."

"But Jake was more than a football player. In the locker room, you'd see him encouraging players to get good grades so they could stay on the team. He offered to help with any subject—it didn't matter what subject you were struggling in, if Jake knew, he offered to be your tutor. I think he personally kept three or four players on the team because of his help."

"He led by example. He didn't complain when we had to do extra drills or when things didn't go right. He learned from his mistakes and did better the next time. Jake taught us how to live our lives because he was always positive and upbeat. He found the good in people and didn't focus on the bad."

"I loved him like a son. In fact, I hope my two boys grow up to be just like Jake Peterson—strong, kind, and caring of others. Thank you," coach said in tears as he left the microphone and sat back in his chair.

I was honored by coach's words.

The crowd didn't know how to respond. Should they clap?

Slowly a few people started clapping and then the entire audience clapped. Some cheered. It was humbling to see and feel their support.

Ms. Parker was up next. She had some notes written on blue index cards that she brought up to the podium. She looked at the crowd first before she spoke and admired the hundreds of people gathered.

"I can say that it was truly an honor to know and work with Jake Peterson. He was a natural leader. Good leaders work with their team and Jake did that, day in and day out. He was great with ideas—a very creative type. But he also made sure every detail was done right, on time, and in budget. He's been one of my favorite students for many reasons, but most of all because Jake cared about everyone. He friended the students who had no friends. He supported people who were polar opposite from him."

"He cared about people first and foremost—it didn't matter what grade they were in, if they were conservative or liberal, what their interests were or if they even liked him. He cared about everyone equally. We can all learn from Jake that no matter how someone looks, smells, what part of town they come from, what race they are, how much money they have, or what their political or religious beliefs are, we are all on this earth together and he treated everyone as if they were his best friend."

"Mr. and Mrs. Peterson, I know I speak for the entire student body and faculty when I say we are all so sorry for your loss. The world lost a great guy this week. A leader who left his mark on everyone he met. May we all honor Jake tonight and in the future!"

The crowd erupted into cheers and applause as she turned to walk back to her seat.

Up next was Chandler. He wore my football jersey #50 in my honor. He struggled to get out of his chair—leaning over as he cried. He got up with tears in his eyes and a heavy heart.

"Jake was my best friend," he started with a crackling voice and sniffles. "We did everything together. From the time we were in kindergarten, we were always in the same classes and always spent time together. I loved him like a brother. He was the brother I never had. And I will miss him so much."

"There are many things we can learn from Jake's death. For starters, let's all commit to never drink and drive."

Cheers came from the crowd. Sackcloths cheered especially loud at that statement.

"Let's also commit to treat everyone with respect and kindness. And let's help the people who are not so popular, not so smart, and not so cool. That's what Jake would want.

"Next is the candlelight part of the candlelight vigil," he said with a bit of a smirk on his face for trying to be funny to break up the sadness of the night. "Each of you has been given a candle. There are faculty members with lighters who will now come around to help you light your candles. When your candle is lit, please use it to light the candle next to you. When enough candles are lit, the stadium lights will turn off except for a few emergency lights."

As Chandler spoke, people lit their candles. Soon there were hundreds of lit candles, and the stadium lights turned off. The candles glowed in the night sky.

Chandler waited another minute. "Everyone please hold your lit candle up in the air."

"Tonight, we honor the life of Jake Peterson. He was a great guy. A football player. The senior class president. A straight-A student. And a friend to all. Jake was a good person. He didn't break the rules. Heck—he didn't even bend the rules. When other guys were making mistakes, Jake was doing the right thing. Always. Sometimes that got annoying."

The crowd laughed. And so did I.

"So tonight, as a celebration of his life, I challenge everyone to be more like Jake. Do the right thing. If you want to show respect to Jake Peterson, then please show kindness to all.

"We will now have a moment of silence for each of you to remember Jake in your own way."

Chandler paused.

You could hear sniffles and crying in the crowd.

And I felt such love from everyone there.

That moment of silence lasted about two minutes. When Chandler said "thank you," the lights came back on.

Principal Evans got back up to end the ceremony. "I want to remind everyone that Jake's funeral is this Saturday morning at 10 at the Bonita Del Sol chapel located at 2121 Evergreen Street. I've been asked to encourage car-pooling as it is expected to be a large crowd. Now, as we end this ceremony, we ask that you please blow out your candle and deposit them in the trash cans at the exits of the stadium. We will see you all at the funeral Saturday."

CHAPTER 21

THE PROTEST

The following night was the night the extreme sackcloths were going to protest outside Katie's house. They made signs that said "Murderer!" and "God will punish Katie!" and "Justice for Jake!" It was a stark contrast from the love everyone felt and heard at the candlelight vigil.

By nine p.m., there were dozens of sackcloths protesting outside the Martin home. They had waited until it was completely dark to start the protest, to improve their chances of hiding their identity.

Having this many extreme sackcloths gathered together in one place was unusual. They usually hung out in smaller groups. But this sin was so grievous that they were there in large numbers and kept coming. They were dressed in all black with a piece of sackcloth as a belt or headband. Most painted their faces or wore a ski mask.

They were a scary looking bunch. They were motivated to deliver a message, and they planned to do it with force and destruction.

Katie's parents were home as the protestors were circling the street in front of the Martin home. They were shouting "Katie is a Murderer!" They wanted everyone in the neighborhood to hear them. And being such a small neighborhood, everyone that was home heard them.

"What do we do?" asked Hannah, as she peaked through the shutters to get a look at the crowd in hopes they didn't see her.

"Let's give them a few minutes, and maybe they will go away," Jeff said.

Katie's parents turned out all the lights, as if they were going to bed, but that made the sackcloths yell louder.

A couple sackcloths brought spray paint and painted "MURDERER" on the side of the Martin's house in huge letters.

Then, they poured gasoline on the Martin's yard in the shape of a cross and lit it on fire.

That's when Katie's dad called the police. They were scared about what a big crowd of protestors could do to them physically. But the police said other neighbors had already called, and they had two police cars on their way.

As the protestors got more violent, the sound of the police sirens could be heard in the distance. Many of the protestors left when they heard the sound. A few, trying to send a final message, picked up rocks and threw them at the Martin's home, shattering multiple windows and then ran into the darkness of the night.

Jeff grabbed his shotgun and headed for the door.

"No," Hannah said to him.

"We have to protect ourselves," he said, loading bullets into the gun.

Just then, two police cars pulled up with sirens blaring and the rest of the crowd dispersed. Cops got out of their cars and chased after a few sackcloths, tackling a couple in the grass behind the Martin home.

Out of 30 or 40 protestors, only three were caught. The rest got away, as they had planned their escape route well and implemented it at the first sound of the sirens.

But the sackcloths delivered their message. And the people in Bonita Del Sol had another tragedy to deal with—not knowing when this mob would come back and what they would do next.

CHAPTER 22

THE FUNERAL

My funeral was held that Saturday. Every deceased person gets to be present at their funeral. I floated down early by myself and spent some time floating above everyone, watching people as they parked and came into the church.

The sun was shining, birds were singing, and people had come from all over to show their support to my family at this difficult time.

My grandparents said they would be there when it started. Making the trip down to earth by myself was cool. I felt important and independent.

I was amazed at the number of friends who showed up. I was also amazed at the number of police who attended, to stop the potential of any violence that would have been caused by radical sackcloths. After the protest at Katie's house, the city was on high alert.

In my church there is usually an open casket viewing before a funeral service, but my body was so badly mangled that my face was not recognizable, even after multiple hours of work by the funeral staff. My mom wanted people to remember me the way I always looked—not beat up beyond recognition. I appreciated that. So they had a closed casket viewing with a large photo of me on top of the casket.

In addition, there were pictures of me all over the room, from my early childhood, through school, to graduation. There was even a picture of me and Katie from prom that was posted after much discussion, but my mom said that Katie was a big part of my senior year, and we all needed to forgive her. What a great example my mom is to so many people.

To think that my parents could forgive her after she took my life showed how humble and loving they were. They knew it was an accident and knew Katie would struggle with this for the rest of her life without any added pain our family could cause her. Even if Katie knew of their forgiveness, that would only give her a little comfort for what would eat at her for the rest of eternity.

You never realize what people really think of you until your funeral. During the viewing, I overheard people talking about little things I had done for them and how much it meant to them: a freshman girl whose books I helped pick up once; a couple of guys who I loaned lunch money to; football players who said I taught them how to be tough. Teachers told my parents what a good kid I was. Even some people I didn't agree with said they respected me. A lot of people called me a "rule keeper." I didn't think of myself as that, but I guess I always tried to do the right thing.

Sometimes you go through life oblivious to the affect that you have on people's lives. It made me wish I had another chance at life on earth. I would have tried harder to make people happy and to do more things for other people because in the end, that's all that really matters. But you don't get a second chance at life.

Katie's parents had posted bail and her attorney asked the judge for permission to attend the funeral, which he granted. When she walked in the door of the church, time seemed to stop. She came with her parents, but she looked so lonely. When she entered the church, everyone instantly became silent—even the organist who was playing some soft music stopped when she saw her.

Everyone looked at Katie. A few radical Sackcloths were staring her down. Many people talked negatively about her, pointing at her, and criticizing her and her family for what she had done.

Katie felt the weight of everyone staring at her. Luckily, the organist resumed playing the prelude music again and most people eventually focused on the funeral—and not Katie. Most were shocked she was there—partly because they didn't know she'd be allowed to attend and partly because they didn't think she should have the right to attend the funeral of the person she killed.

Many people—even some good Christian people—gave her the evil eye, as they watched her find her seat. That pierced her heart like a sword. She was a sobbing mess before she got to her seat, but the reality of the funeral and the tension she felt added much more trauma to her already overwhelming day. Seeing how totally devastated she was, I felt so bad for her. I really did love her, and I didn't want her to hurt so much.

To not be any more of a disturbance than she already was, she and her parents took a seat in the back of the church. But even sitting between her parents on the last row, Katie was very noticeable and uncomfortable. And that's exactly what the judge had hoped for.

My grandparents arrived and waved at me as they floated through the roof but went right over to my parents and family to comfort them. They have been such a blessing through this whole situation—both for me and for my family.

Other spirits came too and floated overhead. Most of them were the relatives whom I met when I first ascended to heaven. There were my great grandparents on both sides—Peterson's and Thatchers, and great-great grandparents too.

Then I saw a familiar spirit face. "Spirit Chandler!" I said. "It's great to see you here."

"I got special permission to come down and be here to support you and your family."

"Thank you for being here. See the guy at the front with the red tie?"

"Yes."

"That's my best friend – Chandler. The one you remind me so much of."

"That's great. Where's your girlfriend?"

"There" I said, pointing to Katie on the back row.

"That's tough, man. How's she handling the situation?"

"Not well. But I totally understand."

"Still love her?"

"Yes," I said quietly.

"Everything will be ok," he said. "I'm going to go float around for a bit and let you do your own thing. I'll catch up with you later."

"Thanks again for being here with me."

A couple dozen spirits attended my funeral—almost all relatives. They hovered in the air above the congregation. Some were still while others floated back and forth a bit.

I floated over to Katie again.

When the service started, I was still gazing at Katie and feeling so sad for her. As I floated around her, I kept thinking how awesome she was. I missed her so much.

After spending time with Katie, I floated close to my family on the front row. They were all dressed in black. My mother was struggling with my loss but with a reassurance that I was ok after our experience in the funeral home. My brother and sister were doing as well as can be expected. My dad was quiet and reflective. They had all suffered so much this week. I think there comes a time in the grieving process when you just can't cry any more. My dad had reached that point. The rest of the family was close.

The priest conducting the service could barely get the words out, as he announced the program. No one from my family wanted to speak. They said the pain was too great. Knowing that, my friend Chandler offered the eulogy.

"This is something I never thought I'd have to do," Chandler said with tears running down his face.

"Jake Peterson was my best friend. He and I, and Tyson and Ben…well, we did everything together. I still can't believe he's gone." Collecting himself he continued. "Jake grew up here in Bonita Del Sol his whole life. He attended Franklin Elementary, Jenson Park Junior High and West View High School. Jake was a smart guy, getting straight-A's in most classes without trying much. We hated that about him!"

The audience laughed at that.

"In every grade, everyone loved Jake. He was a friend to everyone. It didn't matter who you were or who you hung out with or what you did—Jake Peterson was your friend. He helped people. He motivated his teammates on the football team to play better. And he was always so happy."

"Jake was a good guy. He wouldn't break the rules… in fact, he wouldn't even bend them. And he made sure we kept the rules too. He never got into trouble, and I admired that about him. But that doesn't mean he didn't know how to have fun. He was always fun. He was the instigator of many practical jokes on students. The overflowing toilet prank that happened in the boy's bathroom every other week? Yes, Jake was the mastermind behind that one."

Students laughed. Even a few teachers did.

"He loved life. He always had fun and was the life of the party. That's just one of the reasons everyone wanted to hang out with Jake Peterson."

"I've asked many friends to tell me what they will remember most about Jake, and the response was overwhelming. Here are just a few:"

"He was always nice to me, even when other students were not."

"Jake was the most handsome guy in school."

"Jake was so happy all the time that I thought he was always up to something."

"He was a great football player who motivated me to play better."

"He was a rad dude."

"We went to Junior Prom together, and I know every other girl was jealous."

"Great body!"

"He was a true leader in everything he did."

"So glad he was our senior class president."

"He made senior year more memorable."

"I could go on and on and on. But you're here because you already know Jake was that great. He was better than everyone else—but he never acted like it. I think he was smarter than most—but he never acted like that either."

"His life ended on June 12, in a tragic accident." Chandler paused and held back more tears. It took a minute for him to regain composure—especially when his eyes met Katie's eye in the back of the room. She was sobbing quietly between her parents."

Some people looked back at Katie after he said that, as if to reinforce the crime she had committed.

"Jake was a good Christian," he continued, "and you knew it by the way he lived his life. Everything he did was good. And because of that, he was the happiest guy I knew. If we learned anything from Jake, it was that we should do good to others and not hate. Life is too short to be angry or offended or treat others unfairly or with disrespect. We should assume the best in people, not the worst. That's what Jake did."

"Each of us should honor Jake Peterson by ending the anger and hatred we have, doing good deeds to others, and showing love to everyone: regardless of our differences. Let's all do that to honor Jake. I know I will."

When Chandler told people to honor me, I saw many heads nodding, and I could feel a change coming over the hearts of many in attendance.

Looking down at the casket, he continued: "Love you man. You will always be my best friend."

He sat down with tears in his eyes.

There was a musical tribute next. My high school choir sang "Where Can I Turn for Peace?" and it was inspiring. There was not a dry eye in the building after that.

A prayer was given next, by my friend Ben. It was a rehearsed and written down prayer, but Ben still struggled through it.

Up next was my priest who spoke about the afterlife. He used a lot of Bible scriptures. It is interesting to hear what people on earth think about life after death, compared to what I now know.

The priest talked about me being with my grandparents who had died a few years ago, saying that they greeted me at heaven's door and were reunited with me in a joyous reunion. He was right about that!

He encouraged everyone to prepare themselves for Heaven by being the best version of themselves on earth. He read scriptures about the life of Jesus and what Jesus did to show love to everyone.

As he continued, I found myself floating to the back of the church to be near Katie again. I floated around her.

I wished she could see me. I wished I could tell her everything would be ok. And I wished I could comfort her as she was so messed up by this entire situation.

I was caught up with Katie for the rest of the service. When it ended, I realized I had not paid attention to the last 10 minutes or so because I was completely focused on Katie.

At the end, my family was dismissed first. I looked at each of them. They were still struggling and crying. That was hard for me. I wanted to tell them all that I was ok. I floated around them so perhaps they would feel my presence. My mom paused for a second as she was walking out—a sign that maybe she felt me near her again. That brought a slight smile to her face... and to mine.

I wondered what my family would be like without me in it. I thought of how things would be different at home. I floated around Zack and Jane, feeling bad for the pain and suffering they went through this week at such young ages.

They got into a limo that the funeral home provided to drive them to the cemetery. I stayed in the limo with them to provide any comfort I could. They were all silent for a while. Then, my mom broke the silence.

"It was so great to see so many of his friends there today," she said.

"Yes, it was," dad said quietly.

"Why did Katie come?" my sister asked.

"Katie was a big part of Jake's life," dad said. "She was paying her respects to Jake."

"But she's the one who killed him!" Jane said angrily.

"Honey, we need to let God judge her. We just need to try to show love," my mom said.

"I don't think that's possible," Jane said.

"It may not be right now. But hopefully sometime in the future you can. That's the right thing to do."

"I don't know."

"Give it time dear."

And then they got quiet for the rest of the way to the cemetery.

As we drove, I looked at each family member and felt great compassion for each one. My dad was quiet and contemplative. I could tell he was thinking about how life would go on. I loved that man and all he did for me on earth. I don't know if I ever told him how grateful I was that he was my dad. Now I didn't have that opportunity.

I stared into the eyes of my little brother Zack. I could tell he was confused by it all, asking questions like where I was, why I had to die now, and how my family would get through it all. As a spirit, you can sense what people are feeling and thinking. I felt a strong love from my brother. We always got along fine, but given our age gap, I never did much with him outside of family trips. I regretted that now.

Jane was a mess. Still weeping, she had buried her head into mom's lap and was likely ruining her dress with her tears. My mom ran her fingers through Jane's hair to comfort her.

I saw the despair in my mom's face most of the morning. She lost her eldest son. Tragically. That's a lot for a parent to take. Mom was super strong though. I knew her mind was still unsettled by my death, but I also knew she had felt my presence a couple times and she knew that somehow things would work out. It helped her to know I was safe and happy. She had a peaceful look on her face that told me she was either feeling my presence again or thinking of the good times we had as a family.

As I floated there in the car with them, I felt such a strong love for each of them. I spent every day of my life with them. I hope they knew how much they all meant to me. When you're living on earth, you don't always take the time to tell people how grateful you are for them. I wish I could do that now.

The limo parked at the cemetery, and my family waited for the driver to open the door. Even then, with the door open, they moved slowly as if they didn't want to get out. Afterall, this was the end—the burial.

The cemetery was beautiful with lots of trees lining the perimeter and a few large trees throughout the grounds. Most everyone that came to the funeral came to the burial service too. Even Katie.

I didn't realize she was attending the burial, but at the end of the processional of cars was her parent's car. I quickly floated over to her. She was weeping in the car and didn't want to get out. But she knew she had to.

Once she stepped out, she got more mean looks from those in attendance. She could hear whispers of "why is she here?" and "I can't believe they'd let her come to his funeral!"

Their words were hurtful, but I don't think she could hurt any more than she already did. But still, she was greatly affected by it all.

I spent most of the time floating around Katie, instead of listening to the sermon and prayers during my burial service. I felt such love for Katie, although she caused my death. And I wanted to tell her it was all ok, but I knew she had to work out her repentance with God.

As the priest said the final prayer, I wondered when I'd get to see Katie and my family again. I knew I had to go back when this was over, even though I didn't want to leave.

Katie wanted to tell my family how sorry she was for what happened. Clinging tightly to her mom for support, Katie waited for the crowd to leave. As people left, they all seemed to judge her—at least that's what she thought. Often the guilt we feel makes us believe that everyone is against us. But that's not always the case.

"Can I give Katie a hug?" one of my neighbors asked Hannah.

"Yes, please," she said.

"Oh Katie, I'm so sorry," my neighbor said. "I can't imagine what you're going through. But if you ask God to forgive you, and really, really repent, you can get over this pain," she said.

"Thank you," Katie whispered.

"Hi Katie," said some kids solemnly who walked by her.

"Hi," she replied with more tears in her eyes.

The crowd was mostly gone except for my family, Uncle Ray and Aunt Nancy, and a few other close friends. Then, Katie's parents walked slowly toward my parents.

"Tom and Melissa, we're so sorry for your loss," said Jeff.

"Thank you," my dad said softly.

There was an awkward silence.

"Katie would like to talk to you briefly. Would that be ok?" Hannah asked.

Still my parents were silent.

A few seconds passed but felt like minutes while my parents were processing that they would be getting an apology from the person who killed their son.

"Would that be ok?" Hannah asked again.

My mom and dad looked at each other and mom said "Okay."

Jeff nodded to Katie to come over.

"I don't know if I'm ready for this," my dad said quietly to my mom.

"She needs to heal from this maybe even more than we do," mom said. "And apologizing might be the first step in that process."

I loved my mom. She was so grounded and realistic. She had a great love in her heart and was able to forgive others easier than most.

Katie walked toward my family, but she couldn't look them in the eyes. The way my parents looked at her, I thought it was going to be a major confrontation.

When she came close to my parents, she finally looked up at my mom, and the tears flowed like a river.

She couldn't control her emotions and was speechless for at least a minute, other than the sound of inconsolable crying. And my parents weren't going to start the conversation—they didn't even know if they wanted to have it in the first place.

"I'm…I'm…" Katie stuttered. "I'm so sorry," she finally said with more tears and sobs.

"We know Katie," said my mom, as she reached out to hug her. Mom held Katie for a few minutes. And the awkwardness seemed to dissipate. My mom's hug told Katie she didn't hate her. She hated what Katie did, but didn't hate Katie.

Katie didn't know what else to say.

There was nothing more she could say. She couldn't promise she'd make things better—she couldn't. She couldn't say she'd fix the situation—she couldn't do that either. Taking someone's life is permanent and unfixable. There is no restitution.

The fact that my mother had already started forgiving Katie was humbling to me.

My dad gave Katie a quick hug and said, "Thank you for your apology" while Zack and Jane just looked at Katie with a bit of anger in their eyes. This was my longtime girlfriend. They had loved her. Their anger at her now was the opposite of what they had felt for her just a week ago. Nevertheless, they didn't want to get close to Katie, and she could sense it.

"I need to go now," Katie said. "But I want you to know again how sorry I am."

She looked down at the ground as her mom took her arm and walked away.

Jane, who had been quiet during Katie's apology, had missed her since my death. Katie was like her older sister. Jane was as cold as ice to her, but then, her heart softened a bit. Suddenly, Jane ran to Katie and hugged her. Both of them were in tears as they stood there. Jane didn't understand how she could love someone who she hated for what she did to me.

"I miss you," Jane said.

"I miss you too," Katie said. "I'm so sorry."

They embraced for a minute and then Katie walked away, consumed by the sadness and pain.

And Jane walked back slowly.

My family was ready to go home and mourn together without so many people around. But first, the church was having a luncheon to feed everyone who attended.

They got in their car, and drove out of the cemetery, pausing at the end of the driveway before turning on the main road. They were turning right to go to the church, and as they did, they passed Katie in her parent's car going left.

That separation was very symbolic of two groups going in two different directions with two very different futures.

As I floated around her in her car for a moment, I noticed the pain in Katie's face realizing that her freedom was limited, and she would soon be locked up for a long time.

Being at my funeral made Katie want to change. In the back of the car, she was praying silently to God that He would forgive her, and she silently committed that she would dedicate the rest of her life to Him and choose right over wrong.

Her pleas to God continued in her home that day, where she constantly asked for forgiveness and told God she was going to change her life for Him. She felt great remorse for what she had done—that was obvious. And soon, she was going to spend decades in jail to pay for it.

Some people commit to change conditionally—I'll be good if you'll do this for me. But Katie knew that she had to be good and not ask for anything in return. That was a sign of true repentance. Her sorrow was not conditional. She asked God to forgive her for what she'd done, and she was willing to accept the consequences of her actions no matter what.

That was the right thing for her to do. Her heart and mind were mapping out a plan for her to make restitution for this, to be a more caring person and to bring more religion into her life. She also wanted to speak to high school students about the dangers of drunk driving.

Knowing my time visiting earth was short, I left Katie and quickly floated to the luncheon at the church. My grandparents met me there. The food looked so good—I wish I could have tried everything. Heck, I wish I could have tried anything.

I spent a few minutes hovering by each of my friends. I was impressed that so many of them were committing to each other to live a better life, to help everyone stop the anger, to do good deeds for others and to put God first in their lives. There was a good feeling there.

I spent my final minutes of the luncheon by my family. I tried to let my mother know I was ok again—as I wasn't sure when I'd get to see her again. I got close to her and whispered in her ear that I was ok, and everything would be all right. During a funeral, some people are very in tune with the other side. My mom felt my presence again. I saw her eyes open wider for a second and then the tears streaming down her face.

Our spirits communicated for a brief moment, and I knew that she knew I was here.

"He's ok," she whispered to my dad.

"I'm sure he is."

"No, I really feel that he's here telling us that he's ok. He's happy and has no pain and he wants us to know that everything is going to be ok," she said.

Tears were streaming down my dad's face. "Thank you," he said.

With that successful connection, I knew I could leave and go back to heaven. It was hard to go this time, but I felt that I left them with a good feeling about my situation and their future without me.

As I floated above them, I heard my friend Ben telling some friends that he was not going to break the rules or even bend them... just like me.

Being at your own funeral is hard. Seeing so many friends and family members feeling so sad is painful to take in. But I realize that pain and sorrow are part of life and part of the plan God has for us. It's not God's fault that bad things happen to us—that's just life. If we didn't have challenges, we would never be that strong. Sure, God could stop every bad thing from happening to people on earth. But that wouldn't give us experiences that make us stronger and better. Life isn't about everyone winning a trophy. It's about experiences—both good and bad—that mature us and teach us how to deal with issues.

I reflected on this while I floated back to heaven with my grandparents.

"That was a wonderful funeral Jake," my grandmother said, floating alongside me.

"Yes, what great friends you have Jake, and what a major influence you were to them," grandpa said.

"Thanks. I guess you never realize the impact you have on people until you die," I said.

"That's always the case," grandpa said.

"Do you remember our funeral?" grandpa asked.

"Yes, but I was only 12 years old," I said, looking at the earth now below us and the sunlight.

"We were there for it, and I floated near you to tell you we were ok and that we loved you," grandpa said.

"That was hard for us to see," grandma said. "All the tears."

"Well, you both died at the same time and died so tragically – so tragically that we couldn't even see your bodies. I wasn't totally sure what happened or where your bodies were. That was really hard for me."

"We were ok," grandpa said. "We tried to let everyone know that. Yes, it was tragic, but it happened about as fast as your death did. In a few seconds, we were gone."

"I don't remember if I felt your presence at your funeral or not," I said. "I just remember being so sad for weeks after."

"I know," grandpa said. "Grandma and I visited you often during those weeks to try to bring you comfort.

"Thank you," I said. "It took a while for me to get over it."

By this time, we had floated up to the landing area. I was impressed again by the brightness and beauty of it. I was also impressed by how busy it was. Spirits were everywhere. Floating, teaching, greeting, and serving. They were always doing things.

CHAPTER 23

GETTING TO WORK

A few days had passed since my funeral, although I don't think earth and Heaven are on the same clock. There's no nighttime like earth—we don't get tired because we have no bodies, so we don't sleep. But we are aware of each new day on earth as we are given assignments and responsibilities to care for our loved ones.

"What are we going to do today?" I asked my grandparents.

"I heard we are going to get another assignment today either from our group leaders or the legion heads," grandma said.

"Legion heads?" I asked.

"All angels are assigned to be in groups of about 1000 spirits," grandma said. "Each group has leaders—usually a couple. One hundred groups of angels make a legion. And every legion has leaders, usually a head angel couple."

"So that's 100,000 angels in a legion," I said.

"You always were a smart one," grandpa said.

"But how many legions are there?" I asked.

"Thousands," grandma said.

"Wow! There are that many angels up here?" I asked.

"Of course," grandma said. "Think of the billions of people that lived on the earth before you, and the billions that were born after you," she said.

"It feels like a big family," I said.

"We all came from the same God, which makes us all brothers and sisters," grandpa said.

"I know. I wish everyone on earth realized that. Maybe they'd get along better than they do."

Just then our group leaders floated up to us.

"Hello Rex and Cathy, and Jake," said the male group leader. "Jake, I'm Carson Scott, and this is my wife Amy," he said confidently and with love.

"It's great to meet you," I said.

"How are you settling in?" Carson said.

"Great," I said. "But I don't think I have any other option but to be here."

They laughed.

While grandma and grandpa greeted him, I was admiring him and his wife.

They looked like the power couple. No wonder why they were our group leaders. He had an abundance of confidence but communicated with love. I could tell that he was the type of guy on earth that was probably a great public speaker and had a lot of friends. His body glowed like a lantern, as he hovered slightly above us. Amy was attractive, confident, and very kind. Just looking into their eyes made you feel loved.

"We're here with an assignment for the three of you," Carson said.

"Jake, this is a tough assignment," Amy said. "Even though every assignment is different, you'll feel great satisfaction to be able to go back to earth and help people in need."

"Rex and Cathy, we received information that your son Ray is in a situation and needs some help," Carson said looking at grandma and grandpa.

"Sure, what's up?" grandpa said.

I was amazed at the experience, wondering what my Uncle Ray had done that required intervention from heaven.

"Right now, he's home alone and his wife and children have gone out of town for the weekend," said Carson. "He's invited his secretary to his house tonight and has bad intentions with her."

"Nancy and the kids left right after my funeral to go the beach for the weekend to get away from everything," I said. "But Ray said he had too much work to do and needed to stay home..."

My Uncle Ray thought he was a lady killer. He was a decent looking 40-year-old guy and a big flirt. I know it bothered my aunt Nancy that he flirted with every good-looking woman, but she was too kind and quiet to say anything to him. I was disappointed in Ray. What was he thinking? Why would he even consider cheating on Nancy? Or anyone. Nancy was so good to him. Too good for him.

"We need you to go down and be a good influence on his spirit to make the right choices," Amy said.

"Got it," grandpa said. "We'll leave immediately."

"Let's go Jake," grandpa said lovingly. "We'll explain on the way."

Grandma and grandpa had received assignments like this before. The three of us went to a departure platform, checked in with the sentinel and soared back toward earth at rapid speed.

I was amazed that my grandparents were not angry at Ray. At least not yet…

"Jake, this is a big part of our responsibility," grandma said. "When our loved ones on earth are facing major temptations or challenges, sometimes, we are asked to help."

"But how are we physically going to help Ray if we're only spirits? We can't kick his secretary out of the house," I said, as we floated closer to earth.

"No, we can't, but that's not what we were asked to do," grandma said. "Everyone still has their freedom to choose. We're going to put the right thoughts in Ray's mind and hope that our influence helps Ray come to his senses and change his mind."

"I'd like to kick Uncle Ray in the crotch, in hopes it would knock some sense into him," I said.

"Now Jake," grandma said.

"Jake, we are called to be a positive influence on him. That's all we can do," grandpa said.

"How do we do that?" I said, willing to help anyway I could.

"Remember the cartoons with a person who had an angel on one shoulder and the devil on the other?" grandpa asked.

"Yes."

"That's what we're going to do. We're going to whisper to Ray's spirit that he's making a huge mistake," grandpa said. "Just like when you told your parents in the funeral home that you were ok. We hope Ray acts on our message and has a change of heart."

"Will the devil be there too?" I asked.

"There is already an evil spirit there influencing him to make this choice," grandma said. "Evil spirits stay on earth constantly and try to influence people to do bad things. We just need to see if we can get Ray to listen to us instead of following the evil spirit."

I was amazed at the thought of sending a message into Ray's heart that he should not have an affair. Giving comfort to my parents is one thing but getting someone to change their mind seemed like an impossible task.

I wondered how effective it would be. What would we say? And what if we fail? Are we going to be responsible for his adultery if we can't convince him? I don't want to fail and cause him to have an affair with his secretary.

As our assignment sunk in, I felt a sense of dedication to helping others make good choices. We couldn't make the choice for them, but our job as angels was to put the right thoughts in their head to help them choose the right.

We quickly landed at Ray's house. The night was calm. The lawn was freshly mowed, and he had already turned on the party lights on the back porch. He lived in a moderate home, but it was well-cared for and in good condition.

We always loved going over there for barbeques because he had a big grassy backyard. We played for hours while the adults sat on the porch talking and watching the sun set.

Now, that memory was being replaced with the thought of what Ray was planning to do there.

As we floated through the walls of his house, we saw Ray getting things ready for his visitor.

Ray had romantic jazz music on throughout the downstairs and in the backyard. He was cleaning up the house, running around getting things to look good. We floated upstairs to his bedroom. We saw he had made his bed. I wonder if he ever made the bed, I thought.

On the bed, he had neatly pressed clothes—what he planned to wear that night. He had freshly cleaned shoes on the floor. With Nancy gone, he was clearly up to something.

"We have to wait until Ray is still and quiet," grandma said. "The efforts of angels are not as effective with loud music and stress. It's during quiet moments when people are more in tune with angelic inspiration," she said.

"Jake, why don't you just observe for a bit," grandpa said. "Then you can jump in later."

"OK."

My grandparents followed Ray, as he went through the house tidying up. When he walked upstairs, the music was much softer, and he was only focused on changing a shirt and getting ready for his visitor. As he was looking in the mirror, he paused for a minute and whispered, "What the hell am I doing?!" That's when my grandparents jumped at the chance.

Grandma and grandpa were circling around Ray's head, floating within a few feet of his head, and looking into his eyes. This wasn't the angel-on-the-shoulder technique I saw on TV.

Then, after a couple circles around Ray's head, grandma said loudly, "Ray, why are you doing this? You know it's wrong!"

That startled me. It was loud for me, but of course, Ray couldn't hear anything. It wasn't a shout, but a very direct and loud message delivered with love.

She spoke to him like two people that are alive would speak to each other. But he couldn't hear her and didn't show any sign that he got the message.

"Ray, you love Nancy. Don't hurt her," grandpa said loudly. "Think of her and the kids. Don't hurt them!"

Can he hear us, I wondered…?

"Ray, don't make this mistake, it will ruin your marriage and your life," grandpa said. "Think of the kids."

"Think of Nancy," grandma said. "NANCY! NANCY! You made a commitment to Nancy!"

They continued to speak these messages to Ray, hoping to get his good side to overcome his bad side. After a few attempts with no visible impact Ray paused for a second, hopefully to reflect on his feelings.

He sat on the bed thinking. As he stopped for a minute, I wondered if he was aware of the messages we were sending.

Then, we saw a dark cloud blanket him. It was as if he was surrounded by a thick black cloud ready to dump rain on him. There was a bad feeling in the room.

"What's that?" I asked.

"That's the evil influence we're fighting against," grandpa said.

Ray got up and put on his shoes, tying them slowly.

"I don't think we got through to him," I said.

"No," grandma said. "He's back to thinking about what he's about to do. Evil spirits had influenced him to cheat on his wife for months. This wasn't something that happened overnight."

"Jake, evil spirits took advantage of every time Ray and Nancy had a fight or didn't see eye to eye on things," grandpa said. "That's what they do."

"Those spirits would put doubt in his mind about his marriage, telling him that his marriage wasn't working and that he deserved something better," grandpa said. "They deliver these types of messages consistently. Then, when an opportunity arises like his secretary showing interest, those evil spirits pounce on it."

"Evil spirits had persuaded him to invite his secretary over," grandma said. "Once they were successful, they moved on to tempt another person. But now they are back to try to finish this."

There is a dark and angry feeling associated with evil spirits. While we can't see them and they can't see us, we can feel their influence and they can feel ours. They knew we were there to influence him to do the right thing. And they weren't happy about it.

Evil spirits filled the room with darkness – not a darkness that blinds your eyes, but a darkness that blinds your spirit, your conscious and your character. We could see Ray getting comfortable with the thought of having his secretary over again.

But even with the evil spirits in the room, my grandparents didn't let up.

"Be smart Ray!" grandma said.

"Remember Nancy. Don't hurt Nancy or the kids," said grandpa.

We stayed with him and kept sending the message over and over again. We knew the evil spirits were equally sending messages for him to go through with it.

Grandpa finally shouted at Ray "pick up the phone and cancel with your secretary. Cancel her, Ray!" He kept sending that message to Ray to pick up his phone.

You could almost see the emotional struggle Ray was having. This secretary had been showing him the attention he felt he was not getting at home. The evil spirits had been working on him for months to get him to this point, telling him that Nancy didn't really love him and he deserved better.

"Join us Jake," grandpa said. "Let's all three shout at him to cancel this date."

"CANCEL YOUR DATE, RAY!" We shouted it multiple times right near his head.

We all looked him in the eyes when we said it.

Then Ray paused for a second. He shook his head.

We weren't sure what he was thinking—if he was shaking us off, or the evil spirits.

Ray grabbed a photo of Nancy and the kids from his dresser and stared at it for a while. Then, he let out a big sigh as he put it back down.

Then, to our surprise, Ray picked up his phone and dialed.

"Well, hello," said the woman in a sexy voice.

"I'm not sure if I'm ready for this," Ray said.

"Oh, come on Ray, it will be ok."

Ray paused for a second. Was he going to cave to her? "No. I'm sorry," Ray said. "I can't go through with this right now."

"We may never get a better chance," his secretary said.

"I realize that," Ray said. "But I just can't tonight. I'm not as ready for this as I thought I was."

Grandma smiled as Ray said that. "Let's go," she said.

"But don't we need to stay to make sure he doesn't change his mind?" I said.

"No. He's fine," grandma said. "We were successful in changing his heart tonight. Let's hope he continues to question and challenge the evil influences around him."

We began floating away, through the roof (which I loved doing) and upward toward heaven. I was amazed at what we just did. We saved their marriage. Tonight. Just like that.

"You did great, Jake," said grandpa.

"We're a good team," I said. "How often are you called back to earth to do things like that?"

"We go back to earth as often as needed—sometimes only once or twice a week, but other times it can be 10 or 12 times," grandma answered. "It's a wonderful opportunity to help our loved ones get through challenging times."

"Is it always to help someone avoid evil?"

"No," said grandma. "Sometimes we go to give comfort to family members who are sad, lonely, or depressed. Sometimes we are called to save someone from danger. Sometimes we have to let things happen, like in your situation. We wanted to help, but it was your time."

"Whatever the assignment, it is always very rewarding," grandpa said.

He was right. I felt a sense of accomplishment, like I had done something great. What we did benefited their whole family, and the way I felt, I could tell God was pleased with our actions.

As we floated back to Heaven, our group leaders Amy and Carson were waiting for us. They asked for a report and my grandparents did all the talking. They told the group leaders that it took a while, but Ray finally called off his date and they felt he might realize he can work through his marital problems. The group leaders were pleased. They thanked us.

"Don't forget that we'll be practicing for the Second Coming later," Amy said.

"Practicing what?" I asked.

"All the spirits have been practicing for our role in the Second Coming," Amy said. "There are big plans for that day that all spirits are needed for. We have a huge processional of angels that float in a circle down to earth and sing in unison to God."

"Wow," I said. "That sounds so cool!"

"Oh, it is," Carson said. "And we can't wait for you to join us. We'll see you there in a bit."

"Tell me more about this singing and floating thing," I asked my grandparents.

"Well Jake, here's what we know," grandma said. "When the Second Coming happens, God wants legions of angels to light up the sky for everyone on earth. We're going to float down to earth in a huge circle that gets wider and wider as we get closer and closer to earth—kind of like opening the sky. We'll be singing loudly, and we've been told on that occasion, God will make sure everyone on earth hears us."

"Then, when He's ready, the Savior will float down through the middle of that circle of billions of angels and light up the sky brighter than it's ever been before. That will be the start of the Second Coming."

"It will be amazing," I said.

"Oh, it will be Jake," said grandpa. "Everyone on earth will see it, hear it, and feel it."

As we talked, we saw thousands of angels floating to a certain area. Usually, spirits are dispersed all over heaven, but large groups of them were headed toward an open field.

"It's time to go to practice, Jake," said grandpa.

We all floated to the practice area. The practice area was nothing more than a grassy field that was easily the size of 20 or 30 football fields. Every one of the 1000 spirits from our group was there in one corner. There were other groups of angels congregating in other areas on the field too. Each group was doing their own song practice, but everyone was singing the same song.

Singing in heaven was a unique experience. Everyone could sing in tune because they sang with their hearts, not vocal cords.

There was no piano or instruments—just acapella. One choir director was assigned to each group. Our director was a nice woman who taught us by singing to us. And she sang like, well…an angel. Because she was one.

She taught us how to sing loudly by remembering the purpose behind our song. Then, we got to sing. Our first song was mostly hallelujahs. We sang it repeatedly every time she pointed at us. It was magical. Emotional. And full of energy.

I wasn't much of a singer, but somehow in heaven, I had a great voice. I stood by grandpa and sang bass with many other men.

You'd think it would be chaos to have 1000 angels singing without music, but it was organized, efficient, and sounded absolutely incredible.

"Wonderful, absolutely beautiful," said Carson and Amy at the head of the class.

"The plan is for us to sing this hymn repeatedly while floating toward earth," Carson said. "Next, we are going to practice floating in a circle that is 40 miles in circumference. That's one spirit every 220 feet. That may seem like a long distance up here, but when the sky opens for us to do this for real, it will seem small."

"The key is to follow the group leader in speed and distance. The leader will begin to enlarge the circumference of the circle as we descend toward earth. Let's give it a try now."

They taught us how to space ourselves. We lined up and hovered in a line going in a circular motion. We alternated male and female. Most of what we practiced in the circle was floating at a pace that kept the circle spacing uniform. With 1000 angels, uniform spacing should have been a big failure. But this wasn't.

Then we sang the hymn as we floated in the circle. Honestly, it was so impressive that everyone was overcome with joy. It brought a warmth to everyone's soul that helped us know God was pleased with our efforts.

It was unlike anything I'd ever seen or heard.

CHAPTER 24

DISASTERS ON EARTH

A couple weeks after the funeral, Katie pleaded guilty to vehicular manslaughter to get a reduced sentence. The judge sentenced her to 20 years in jail with the possibility for parole after five years. While she and her family knew it was coming, it was still devastating for them emotionally. Katie planned to keep to herself in jail for her protection and self-reflection.

My parents didn't do much for weeks after the funeral. It sucked the energy and motivation out of them. There had been a number of disasters in other countries over the past couple weeks, and my parents were tired of hearing all the bad news.

One night, they were watching TV when a special announcement came on.

"We interrupt this program for a special message from the White House," said the announcer.

"What's happening now?" My dad asked in a tone that showed he was not ready for any other problems.

"I don't know. Let's listen," mom said.

"My fellow Americans, I come to you tonight from the White House with a very important message," said the president. "The Coronavirus has been mostly dormant over the last few years. But when news broke a few months ago that it appeared to be making a comeback, I asked medical staff to monitor it and keep me informed if it became a threat to Americans."

"Over the past few weeks, you've probably heard that Covid seemed to be gaining traction. Medical researchers have determined that the most current strain of the Coronavirus is spreading quicker than initially expected and we have major concerns for the health of all Americans. This new variant is 10 times more deadly than COVID-19. We've already confirmed over 2000 deaths from it in the past couple weeks, and thousands more are sick."

"Unlike COVID-19, this variant is more potent, long-lasting, and lethal. This one has the potential to kill millions of people. It will be especially harmful for the elderly, or those with pre-existing conditions like asthma, diabetes, heart or lung disease, cancers, or leukemia. But it will also be dangerous for babies, children, and teenagers. No one is immune to this—even if you had the vaccine and boosters."

"I have commissioned pharmaceutical companies to work around the clock to develop a new vaccine that will protect us. But it will take time."

"In order to save human lives and keep us from mass casualties, I have asked all Governors to make necessary restrictions that will start as soon as possible—preferably by this Monday. That includes our recommendation for a minimum 30-day quarantine for everyone except essential workers. Your individual governors will announce restrictions for your state very soon."

"This is so serious that we're recommending states issue fines and even jail time for people that break quarantine."

"In addition to state restrictions, we're also restricting travel into or out of America from other countries. The only way we can contain this virus is to stop people from bringing it here from other countries."

"Oh my gosh!" My dad said. "This will be like communism! He's going to kill our economy."

"Unbelievable," my mom said. "But if it will be more severe than the last time, we need to prepare."

"I just can't believe it," dad said.

"The economic devastation could be worse than the medical devastation," mom said. "Thirty days is a long time to keep nearly every American out of work. What does he expect us to do?"

"I know this will be difficult," the president continued. "But it is the only way we can fight this disease and not let it turn into a mass casualty event for our country and our loved ones."

"We need to make a plan," mom said. "We need to stock up on food and supplies."

"Let's get plenty of toilet paper," dad joked. "We should go now." He shut off the TV.

"Good idea," mom replied.

And away they went to the grocery store. But apparently, they weren't the only ones with that idea. When they got to the grocery store, the parking lot was full of other people who felt they'd better stock up too. There were people running into the grocery store as if their lives depended on it.

"I'll drop you off at the door so you can get started, and I'll go find a parking spot," dad said. "Be careful honey!"

"OK," said mom. "Text me when you're coming in and I'll let you know where I'm at."

As she got out of the car and headed in, my dad counted 23 people running in right behind her.

The president's message caused widespread panic because people remembered the problems when Covid-19 was first announced.

Dad couldn't find a parking spot in any row of the parking lot. He drove to the outermost corner of the parking lot and found one spot in the far corner. He parked the car and got out quickly. Soon, he found himself running toward the door too.

As he ran, he saw a big green truck that was circling the parking lot, looking for a bigger parking spot. The driver looked furious and was honking and swearing at all the pedestrians who got in his way.

Dad texted my mom as he ran in the door… and then he saw the pandemonium that had started. People were clearing off shelves of anything they could find—canned goods, produce, frozen foods. Everything.

People in the alcohol section were taking every bottle of liquor they could fit in their shopping bags.

The sound of police sirens could be heard, as it sounded like every police car in Bonita Del Sol was dispatched to help keep the peace all over town.

Mom texted dad telling him she was in frozen foods, but my dad couldn't get there due to all the people in the store. When people are panicked, they do crazy things.

Dad said "excuse me" to everyone in his way, but he couldn't make any progress toward getting closer to my mom. It was a madhouse of panicked people grabbing any food they could get their hands on.

"Get out of my way!" one man yelled at him.

"Calm down," a lady said to the man sternly.

"Help me!" cried an older lady who had been pushed to the floor.

As my dad reached to the floor to help the older lady, the store windows came crashing in as the big green truck crashed through the store windows, shattering them, and sending glass everywhere.

Screams were heard throughout the store. Some customers in line ran out of the store with their food, without paying. Some workers left too, and that's when it became a free-for-all and instantly, everyone was looting.

The man in the green truck jumped out of the truck swearing at everyone for taking all the parking spaces. Then he too ran to the aisles and took as much food as he could.

There were injured people on the ground from the truck, but no one seemed to care. People were running over each other, pushing and yelling as if they were going to die without a few extra cans of soup. My dad helped the older lady up and asked if she wanted help going to her car.

"But I haven't paid yet," she said.

"I'll pay for you," dad said. "We need to get you out of here now."

"OK," she said, recognizing the severity of the situation.

Dad helped her toward the door and called my mom as he did. "Honey, are you ok? Where are you?"

"I'm headed toward the door on the right," she said. "We need to get out of here."

"I'm helping a lady out the door. I'll meet you outside," dad said.

Even though many people left, there were still hundreds in the store, and they were jammed together.

Dad pushed the older lady toward the door by having her stand on the back of her cart. That provided some protection for her from other reckless shoppers. He was as polite as he could be, but also very aggressive in getting her out the door.

Right outside the door was my mother.

"Tom! Over here," she said.

He raced to her with the old woman on the back of his cart.

"I'm so glad you're ok," she said with the look of shock on her face. "I was worried."

"I was worried about *you*," dad said giving her a quick hug. "Worried you were going to get crushed."

The people who were most afraid of the virus were still filling their carts and wouldn't leave. At least until everyone heard police sirens in the parking lot, and then, they got scared and all ran to the doors at once.

"Where's your car, ma'am?" dad asked the elderly lady.

"Right here in the handicapped spot," she said.

They made a beeline to her car.

"Tom, why don't you drive her to her house, and I'll follow you," mom said.

"Good idea," dad said. "I'll drive you to our car."

Mom and dad took over like they do—dad threw the lady's groceries in the back seat while mom helped her get in her car.

"Thank you so much," she said. "You saved my life! Both of you!"

"What's your name?" he asked grabbing her keys and starting her car as fast as he could.

"Bonnie," she said trembling. "Bonnie Parks. Nice to meet you."

"Don't worry Bonnie, we'll get you home safe," dad said.

Cars were speeding out the parking lot, but my dad was able to drive Bonnie's car to where he had parked and let mom out.

"Follow me close," he said. "And don't worry about stop lights—we need to get to safety."

Mom ran out of Bonnie's car and right to her door, dropping her purse in the process and spilling everything. Between the panic of everything, the police cars sirens blaring, and the trauma she'd seen, she picked up her wallet and car keys and jumped in the car, leaving everything else on the ground… including a picture of me she had kept in her purse since my death.

She put the car in reverse and was quickly behind dad as they both raced away from the store toward Bonnie's home.

About a mile away from the store, things were much calmer. But their hearts were still racing from the experience.

Bonnie Parks lived in an older part of town that was surprisingly quiet. Dad parked her car in the driveway, grabbed her groceries and helped her to the door.

"Thank you so much," she said. "You're a saint!'"

"I don't know about that, but thank you," dad said. "Please be careful."

Then dad jumped in the car with mom, who had moved to the passenger's seat as she wanted him to drive. When he got in, she broke down and cried.

"What was that?" she said with tears running down her face from the drama.

"We're lucky to be alive," dad said putting his arm around her. "And we didn't get any groceries," he realized.

"We'll order online tonight," mom said.

They were silent for a bit, letting the situation sink in. At that moment, they both felt the severity of what was going to happen next. With grocery store shelves cleared, a killer disease spreading, people panicking and a mandatory 30-day quarantine happening soon, they realized things were going to be tough. Little did they know, this was just the start. And it was happening throughout the world.

In jail, Katie heard the news about the quarantine and instantly became concerned about her family.

But her thoughts were not panic-driven, as she was clueless to the level of panic, looting and destruction that was happening all over the country.

Katie had spent days thinking about what she had done and the severity of it. She had been praying and pouring out her heart to God, asking Him to forgive her.

She kept thinking of how much she had tried to please her friends instead of doing what was right. She remembered how people always joked that I didn't even bend the rules. What seemed corny then was now something she felt she needed to adapt to her life.

Katie whispered, "I am not going to break the rules, and I'm not going to bend them." It became her mantra and by repeatedly saying it she felt that part of her restitution would be living her life as I tried to live mine.

And while she continued her self-reflection, Americans everywhere were preparing for the quarantine by looting stores and stealing whatever they could to stock up for 30 days of hell. Mass hysteria was everywhere. Some people took guns with them in case they needed extra protection—which caused random shootings across the country.

Sackcloths everywhere were rejoicing, saying the devastation was God punishing everyone. They told everyone to repent because God was coming. But secretly, they were scared too.

Fighting and deaths occurred all over the United States for the next few days. The president called out the national guard to restore peace, but that didn't last long.

People were scared, mad, and overly protective of themselves in a situation that got worse by the day. And it wasn't just in America. All over the world people were killing, looting, hiding, dying, getting COVID, and staying home to prepare for the worst...

CHAPTER 25

PREPARATION TIME

B ack in Heaven, we had two more practices planned for the descension. The first was with every group in our legion. Each group had different space assignments—some were floating in smaller circumferences and some in larger circumferences. Some were below us and some were above us.

At this practice I began to realize the size of this descension. It would be massive!

The plan was there would be legions of angels floating in circles stretching out about 200 miles and upward about 10,000 miles. As each group of angels got to earth, they would float outward, making a bigger circle. From earth, it would look like a descending funnel of angels, growing wider as each row of angels made it to earth.

They assigned groups their location in the circle. We were group 317. There were 316 groups below us and thousands of groups above us. It was massive!

The spacing was specific. From our spacing between spirits in our row to spacing in the rows above and below us—it was all very precise. The result was a sky full of angels with room to move toward earth and yet in a position that it filled the sky with spirits.

Our legion took longer to get into places than our group practice did. But with the help of each group leader, and our legion master, we got there. It was even more glorious than our group practice – 100,000 spirits from our legion, all together in circles on various levels.

With the sign from the conductor, we began to sing. The singing was loud and wonderful. It filled heaven. We sang so loud that I wondered if people on earth could hear us.

After two rounds of the song, we were asked to float in our circle at the desired speed, but without descending.

Again, I thought that task would be complicated, but it went smoothly and sounded like, well, angelic spirits in heaven!

"Well done," the instructor said. "You are all dismissed until we have the entire congregation of legions practice later tonight."

"The entire congregation of legions?" I asked grandpa.

"For the announcement of the Second Coming, almost all legions will be joined together in song and the descension," he said. "It will be a remarkable site to behold."

And he was right.

Later that night, we joined about 200 legions of angels for our practice, and there were thousands of other legions practicing at the same time in other places. While all legions would be joined together for the final descension, tonight we were practicing in smaller groups and then all groups would join together at the time of the Second Coming.

With 200 legions all working together, I thought our practice would surely be chaos. However, it came together smoothly. And when we all began singing, I felt that God Himself was going to appear. It was unlike anything I'd ever experienced or dreamed of.

We only practiced a few times, but the result was almost perfect.

Then, one of the legion masters in charge of the entire experience spoke. "That was absolutely marvelous," he said. "We all felt the love from your singing tonight. And we love all of you so much!"

"We don't know when we'll be asked to perform this final descension, but we know you are all ready, and for that, we thank you."

"Keep in mind that this formation is not a military exercise. While we want to stay in as close of formation as we can, it is not critical that we keep the exact uniformity during the descension."

"If any spirit gets too close or too far away from their spot, just go with it," the lead angel said. "And if one angel has to leave the circle formation for any reason, just move forward and fill in the spot as best you can."

"There are a number of legions that are staying behind to continue operations of receiving the recently deceased. People will continue to die during our descension and will be floating heavenward while we are floating down, so be aware of that during your descension."

"Finally, remember to show love with your eyes, your smile and your song. Let everyone feel the love of God in you."

"Now, carry on with your other work until we get the call for the descension. And when we get the call, we will meet here. Excellent job everyone! We love you."

That practice was so powerful it left most of us speechless. As we floated back, there was a peaceful feeling of what that experience will be like when it happens for real. I stayed close to my grandparents, grateful to have them with me at this moment.

As we left practice, we saw spirit Chandler.

"How'd you like that practice?" spirit Chandler said.

"Great! It was breathtaking!"

"Dude, your breath was already taken away when you died," he joked.

"Oh yeah, huh?!" I said with a laugh.

"This Second Coming is going to be amazing!"

We were quickly interrupted by another visit from Carson, our group leader. "Hi Cathy, Rex and Jake," he said to us. "What a great practice that was!"

"Yes, it was," we all said, almost in unison.

"We need your help with another family member," Carson said.

"Your nephew Sam—Jake, your cousin—is in danger." "He's about ready to go on his break at the hospital and if he walks his normal route during his break, he's headed toward an explosion that could kill him. We need you to divert him from his normal path."

"OK," grandpa said. "We will leave right away."

"Can Chandler join us?" I asked.

"Yes of course, if you're free," the group leader said.

"I'd love to," spirit Chandler said.

The group leaders thanked us, and the four of us hurried toward the nearest launch pad, checked in with the sentinel, and were on our way down to earth in a matter of seconds.

On the way down, I took the opportunity to tell spirit Chandler about Sam. Sam was older than me and had been working at a hospital in Phoenix since he graduated a couple years ago. He was an ER doctor who loved helping people. I always looked up to him because he was smart and was still cool.

With the quarantine in place, and the national guard stopping the riots and looting, there was almost no one else on the streets, so Sam was easy to spot. He was wearing his blue scrubs and matching pants.

"There he is," grandma said.

We saw Sam walking out of the hospital's employee door in the back to go on a walk during his break—a daily thing he did. He walked to take his mind off the stress of the day.

We got a vision of where the explosion was going to take place. It was in an abandoned hotel two blocks from his hospital. It had a burst gas line that was seeping gas throughout the building. As soon as the gas reached a pilot light in the boiler room, the hotel was going to blow.

Sam was walking his normal route—down Second Avenue toward the hotel and then he'd turn right on Eastern Avenue and back down Third Avenue to the hospital. It was one mile walk which today could take his life.

We floated around Sam as he walked, shouting "Turn Around!"

It was great having spirit Chandler around. He joined in the effort to shout at Sam, and he was louder than the three of us.

Sam was listening to music and couldn't sense the message we were trying to send him. He had tuned out everything around him.

"Go another way today!" I shouted at him, trying to send a different message.

Nothing.

We were frustrated but kept shouting at him.

Spirit Chandler floated right in front of his eyes and tried to look into his eyes as he shouted "Turn around Sam! Go another way today!"

Just then, he looked up as if he heard us. He hesitated for a couple seconds.

"It's working," I said. "Let's keep it going. Nice job Chandler."

But then Sam walked into the intersection right next to the hotel. He was waiting for the light to change. We saw this as our chance.

"Sam, turn around!" we said.

A car passed, and Sam saw the intersection was clear, so he walked even though the light was still red.

"SAM! TURN AROUND NOW!" Grandma yelled at him, as he crossed the street and was a few feet from the hotel. "YOU'RE IN DANGER!"

He crossed the street and hesitated another second. And then he decided to turn left, away from the hotel. He didn't wait for the light to change and crossed the street. We got through to him!

But it was too late. At the moment he turned to walk the other direction, the hotel exploded, collapsing its walls, and blowing the doors and windows off the hotel into the street, throwing debris into the air and knocking Sam onto the street with debris falling on top of him and all around him.

The debris crushed cars parked along the street, and even blew into buildings on the other side of the street.

Sam was hit multiple times by the debris, and was cut up and hurt, but he was still alive.

"We failed," I said.

"It's ok, Jake, he's still alive under the pile of rubble," spirit Chandler said. "Look, his feet are moving."

"Glad he's alive, but I'm disappointed that we didn't get him out of harm's way sooner," I said. "He looks badly hurt."

Within a minute of the explosion, members of the National Guard who were nearby came running to the scene. We continued floating above Sam for a minute and saw more movement under the debris. He kept moving his feet and hands.

"He's going to be ok," grandpa said. "We did all we can do, and we need to go back and report," he said.

The four of us floated back up to heaven to report back to our group leaders. I loved having spirit Chandler around. He had become an instant, eternal friend.

CHAPTER 26

DESTRUCTIVE FORCES

T wo weeks after the COVID quarantine, more than 80,000 people died from it in the United States alone. The president was right—this was a killer virus that showed no mercy. This virus was airborne and could live for months in any condition. It spread easily. Many countries were affected by it as well, and the death rates were like something out of an end-of-the-world movie.

Between the disease, the quarantine, natural disasters and overall condition of the world, many people were scared. Those who were prepared, stayed in their homes, and tried to make the situation as normal as possible.

Those who weren't prepared became desperate. Desperate people do desperate things, like steal from others. There were millions of people who had no food to eat. They would break down doors of restaurants and grocery stores to steal food. They'd break into people's homes. Usually, they came armed with a weapon. Usually, a thief with a weapon would succeed in getting food. However, some thieves were shot as they broke into homes before they had a chance to steal or even ask for food.

Even radical sackcloths would steal for food—which is totally opposite of the way they lived. They were the ones who would punish people for stealing, but now they were doing it to survive.

Other people tried reasoning with people—knocking on doors and begging for food. Many normal sackcloths did this. Some people bartered money for food. Some gave other things in exchange for food—work, guns, money, jewelry or almost anything.

When faced with people begging for food, many residents obliged. Some didn't— saying they didn't have enough, and their family would starve if they shared their food.

Fights broke out. Some beggars brought guns and used them. Some residents opened the door with a gun in hand. Many murders were committed. It was total utter chaos.

Bigger cities were affected more than smaller ones, but every city had unprepared people who would beg or steal to survive, and shoot to either protect their home, or to get the food they needed.

People who needed medication to survive couldn't get it. Hospitals were overcrowded. And morgues were overflowing. Cities set up morgues in high school gyms or auditoriums. But even that wasn't enough.

For a few weeks, the receiving platform at heaven's gate was busier than normal. People were dying in mass numbers—from the disease, starvation, from violence, from suicide and from the stress of the entire situation. Even though every newly deceased person was always welcomed to heaven with great love, it was sad to watch the massive number of deaths.

My family was ok. They and many of their neighbors had stocked up food and water to fight off the virus and stay safe at home. They even shared a few items with beggars.

Katie was ok too. Jail was the safest place to be since food was mandated for all inmates and was brought in daily in armored cars. And no person desperate for food thinks of breaking into prison to steal any.

Then earthquakes started. Several of them happened all over the world. Nearly a hundred of them in less than a week. More than a dozen earthquakes hit the United States and affected almost every state in some way. Many were over 10.0, which are the biggest ever recorded. They caused tsunamis, fires, broken waterlines, flooding, the collapse of buildings and homes, gaping holes in the earth, and so much more damage.

They were relentless, shaking the ground virtually non-stop for 10-15 minutes each time. When the shaking stopped, the calm didn't last long, as aftershocks and additional earthquakes happened again soon after.

They were destructive and devastating throughout the world. And while earth was experiencing earthquakes, tsunamis and flooding, the sky seemed to explode like firework shows up in the stars.

After hours of the earth shaking, there were a few hours of calm early in the evening. That's when my family went outside to see the damage.

"Oh my gosh!" said my dad who was first out the door.

My mom came out in tears and speechless.

"No way!" shouted Zack. "Look at the mess!"

Our yard had trees down and shingles from our roof in the yard. Bricks from our chimney had also come loose and fallen. Our basketball hoop was down, and our driveway had huge cracks in it.

As they looked around, they saw fires burning in every direction. Thick black smoke could be seen all over.

"Mom, look at the Stewart's house!" Jane shouted.

While our home had some damage, the Stewart's house across the street was nearly leveled into a pile of rubble. One wall was still standing, but all the others had fallen. It looked devastating.

"I have to see if anyone's home over there," dad said. "Stay here while I go over there."

"Tom, I'm coming with you," mom said.

"It's not safe," he said.

"Then it's not safe for you either," she said worried. "I'll go stand in their driveway while you look around."

"I'll be extra careful."

"Jane and Zack, stay with me," mom said, feeling like she didn't want to leave them in case another earthquake hit. "Stay close to me here while dad looks for the Stewarts."

They walked carefully across the street toward the Stewart's house. The road had long cracks in it that were about six to eight inches wide. It wasn't something you could fall into, but the fact that the ground had separated worried everyone that the cracks might further separate and suck them down into it. Parts of the sidewalk in front of the Stewarts home had deep cracks too.

The Stewart's house and yard, which were always meticulously cared for, were destroyed. All their trees were down in the front yard. The walls of their house were laying in pieces on the ground with beds and couches and other furniture ripped up and turned upside down all over the yard.

The Stewarts had a big house, but it was now a big pile of rubble.

"Mack? Carmen?" dad shouted. "Are you ok? Mack?" Dad moved boards and debris to possibly uncover the family. "Are you guys there?"

There was no response.

"Stewarts!" dad shouted as he moved more debris looking for bodies.

"If they were in the home when the earthquake hit, I doubt they made it," mom said.

"I'm thinking the same thing," said dad quietly.

"Jane, take your brother and go back over to our house."

"I don't want to go," Jane said crying. "I want us to stay together."

Dad kept digging and searching for bodies in the piles.

He saw blood on the ground next to a pile of bricks and knew there was a body under it. He threw bricks off the pile almost violently to expose whoever was below it.

There were hundreds of bricks.

"Let's walk toward the street," mom said, sensing dad might have found a body.

After a minute of throwing bricks off the pile, dad's hands were bleeding from all the bricks he had thrown. But he kept going—throwing brick after brick to expose a body below.

And then, he found it.

The Stewarts dog Charlie was dead on the ground from the weight of the bricks. Dad found a ripped-up blanket nearby and wrapped it around the dog, and then embraced it for just a second.

"Did you find anything honey?" mom yelled from the street.

"Not yet," he said, not wanting to alarm the kids.

He didn't know if anyone was home, but the dead dog made him feel that it was more likely the Stewarts were there too—buried under a pile of debris.

So, he kept digging.

While he was digging, other neighbors had come out of their homes. Some walked toward the Stewarts house to help my dad, but everyone walked carefully to avoid the large cracks in case the earth was going to shake again.

A few guys helped my dad.

The moms and children stayed in the street and were looking at the sky which was getting darker. The moon came up, but the combination of the twilight and smoke made it darker than normal for that time. Mom knew dad's time to find the Stewarts was diminishing quickly. They would have to stop searching soon and wait until tomorrow to find the Stewart family.

With the sky darkening with smoke, the moon looked dark red. It glowed with a red tone to it.

My family saw bright objects floating toward the earth. One landed in the distance, far behind the Stewarts house, with a big crash and a burst of light. It was more of a huge light falling to the ground. Then more kept falling all around them.

"What was that?" asked Zack.

"I don't know," mom said. "Maybe a meteor."

"They are falling from the sky," Zack said.

"From the explosions we saw earlier," Jane said.

"Look over there is another one!" Zack yelled.

"Watch out!" dad yelled. "Here comes one straight at us!"

In the sky was a flaming ball of light. It hurled toward them faster than a fighter jet going full speed.

Dad ran toward mom, Jane, and Zack, careful to miss the cracks in the sidewalk and street. He grabbed the kids and ran back across the street to our house.

Everyone watched as the object got closer and closer to earth. It was a ball of fire or light that was getting brighter as it flew toward us. It looked like it was headed straight for our street, just a little way down from our house. Everyone watched it come down.

Then, *CRASH!* The object landed in the back yards of houses across the street with a loud crash, and an explosion of light. When it hit, small pieces broke off and sprays of fire and light came off it in every direction—but the core stayed bright. It lit up the sky around us as if it was the middle of the day.

"Oh my gosh" mom yelled. "What is that?"

"Are those meteors, Dad?" Zack asked.

Everyone was mesmerized by the glowing object. It looked like a huge meteor. When the sprays of fire ended, everyone approached it cautiously, not knowing if it was going to burst into flames or explode or cause some other damage.

The glowing rock was huge—taller and wider than four or five houses. Even after it crashed, it gave off a bright light. The light was strongest in the center—the core of the light source. But there were lights beaming out of the pores of the rock too, making the entire rock or meteor glow like the lights at a stadium. It lit up the sky in our neighborhood. Everyone who got close had to shield their eyes from the brightness.

Neighbors were inspecting it and taking pictures with their phones, while wondering what in the world these glowing rocks were.

"What are they?" Zack asked.

"They look like pieces of stars," Jane said.

"That's it!" mom said. "Stars! Remember? The Bible said stars are going to fall to the ground in the last days."

"Wow," dad said. "I think you're right."

"They're unbelievable!" Jane said admiring the star more closely.

Everyone was looking at the star as closely as possible without blinding themselves, and were amazed at how big a star must be if this was only a part of a star that broke off and fell to the ground.

The ground started shaking again. Houses were shaking. Even the star was moving.

"More earthquakes!" shouted one of the neighbors who were admiring the stars.

"Everyone get back to your houses!"

This time, it seemed to be centered in Bonita Del Sol. Buildings shook and fell. Homes were destroyed. And the shaking kept going…

The night was long for everyone on my street. Many prayers were said. People who had never prayed before were praying to God to end the destruction.

As aftershocks continued to rock the world, people realized that this catastrophe was not likely to end soon. They sensed the need to hunker down, ration food and continue to pray for an end to it all.

CHAPTER 27

THE DESCENSION

We had practiced the descension many times, with no idea of the date we would be performing it. After the last day of mass destruction, we got the word.

We were floating among the spirits in our group when we saw Carson and Amy approaching quickly.

"It's time," said Carson.

The excitement was energizing, with many angels shouting for joy. It was time for most of the angels to go to earth as the start of the Second Coming. Wow. It was real now. And much of the excitement was because Heavenly Father and Jesus would be living among us in heaven permanently after the Second Coming. I was excited for that too!

I rehearsed in my mind my part in the descension. I knew who I followed, and what and when I was to sing. We were honored to use singing to signal this glorious event as God wanted.

We got in positions and waited for the final call from the lead angel. The joy was so intense that you could feel it everywhere. Just the sight of the billions of angels lined up and ready to go was astonishing. A feeling of love rushed through my spirit as I admired so many spirits ready to go. They were glowing with excitement.

The head of our legion floated to our area and talked with Carson and Amy for just a few seconds, then floated away quickly to the next group.

"Let's go!" came the cry from Carson.

"Are you ready Jake?" said grandma.

"Yes, I'm excited."

"Enjoy this moment," grandpa said. "It will be glorious!"

There was a group of spirits who were assigned to stay behind in heaven to greet the recently deceased. Deceased people kept arriving in heaven by the thousands.

I never wanted to stay in heaven during the Second Coming descension unless my family was going to be arriving. But I was assured they would live through the destruction, so I stayed with the group doing the descension. I was glad I had the chance to be in the group of descending angels who were announcing the Second Coming. I wouldn't want to miss this!

"You ready for the big event?" spirit Chandler said as he floated over to me.

"Yes, you?" I asked.

"I'm staying behind," he said.

"What? But you've been practicing this for a long time. Did you volunteer to stay?" I asked.

"Yes. I found out my mom will be passing on today from all the destruction on earth," Chandler said. "I was given the option of greeting her or participating in the descension. I chose greeting her at the arrival platform."

"Wow," I said, not sure of what I would have done.

"I don't know that she'll want to see me," he said. "But I want her to know I'm ok and I forgive her."

"Chandler, you're a great man! And I'm proud to call you a friend."

"Thanks. Same to you. Good luck with the descension. It will be spectacular!"

"Thanks man. I'll see you afterwards."

"Let's hang out later," he joked.

I floated to my spot and waited next to grandma and grandpa. I watched as other spirits were elated about their role in this momentous event. Some had been waiting for this moment for thousands of years.

The timing was impeccable. Each legion of angels was told when to start their descension precisely so that they would consistently float in a never-ending line of bright glowing spirits.

Our group—#317— floated downward in the same circling motion of the group before us. It was a big circle and it expanded as more legions of angels joined us. We were circling about half of the earth. Our circle was millions of spirits wide and millions tall and growing. It was happy, warm, exciting, and spiritual.

The song which had sounded so spiritual before, was louder and all-encompassing of the air around it.

The energy of the descension was unreal. The feeling was powerful. We were telling the world that Jesus was coming. I could only imagine what our descension looked like from earth!

During our descension, spirits of recently deceased people were floating upward toward heaven. Millions of them! Their natural pull toward heaven took them outside of the descending circle we were making so they wouldn't interfere with it. They were floating up behind us as we were floating down. I looked into the eyes of a few that ascended near me. I could see fear in the eyes of some, while others felt joy or relief from a world full of evil and destruction.

I wondered if some of them thought that this processional of angels in the great descension was the greeting every deceased person sees when they ascend to heaven. I chuckled at that thought.

And then I thought of spirit Chandler, who was waiting to meet his mother after all these years... What would that be like?

As we kept circling downward toward earth, we sang hallelujahs just like we practiced. A lot of hallelujahs. It was unlike anything I'd ever seen or felt on earth.

We floated below the veil of clouds and saw that it was evening on earth. The sky was dark below us but the brightness of legions of angels descending toward earth lit up the sky around us like it was almost daytime. We were hundreds of miles from earth, and it was awesome to watch the night sky light up as we continued our path.

As we moved closer, we knew that people on earth would begin to hear us gradually and the volume would grow louder and louder for them as we moved closer. The sky would also continue to get brighter—very bright—as we descended. I imagine the view for people living on earth was truly fascinating and sensational.

Our efforts were preparing the world for the Second Coming. It was almost magical—unlike anything I've ever seen, felt, or dreamed of. There was joy and much rejoicing.

Amidst my descension, I slowed a bit and admired the experience. I looked all around and was amazed at the majesty of millions of angels launching an event that had been foretold for hundreds of years. There were no classes of people here. No EDM's. No sackcloths. Everyone was equal. The way it should be.

As I was taking it all in, I heard a familiar voice yell "JAKE!!"

It was Katie.

The prison walls fell on her during the last earthquake, and she died. She was floating up to heaven.

Seeing her floating toward me was like Christmas morning. She was so beautiful and glowing. She looked happier than I'd ever seen her.

"Oh my gosh, Katie! I've missed you so much!" I floated out of the circle to see her.

"I've missed you," she said lunging toward me. She floated toward me with great speed and floated right through me.

"That happens all the time," I said laughing.

She laughed too... For a minute. Then she got serious. "Jake, I'm so sorry," she said. "You were right, and I was stupid. I'm so sorry I took your life."

"That's ok."

"No! No, it's not ok," she said seriously.

"Everything is ok. I'm fine. I'm just so glad to be with you again," I said.

I had fallen out of formation in the descension of angels, and they kept circling downward, but I didn't care.

"I've asked God for forgiveness," she said. "I need you to forgive me too. I've repented."

"I know you did."

"How do you know that?"

"Because spirits in heaven are aware of many actions of our loved ones living on earth. Katie, I forgive you completely."

She tried to hug me again, and again she floated right through my spirit.

"Let me show you how we show love here," I said. "Hold up your hand."

"OK," she said, doing it.

We put palm to palm and then made sure every finger of her hand lined up with every finger of my hand. As our spirit hands touched, the warm glow I felt was a connection with her that I had missed so much.

She looked me in the eyes and smiled.

It was magical.

I had missed her. Her face. Her laugh. Her smile. I had been looking forward to the day we would meet again.

The glow from our hands was a bond between us. She was communicating how sorry she was for taking my life. I was communicating that I forgave her. And we were both communicating that we still loved each other. I felt like everything around us stopped so that we could reconnect.

By looking into each other's eyes, we communicated a lot, without saying anything.

After a minute she asked, "Where am I supposed to go now? I want to hang out with you but I'm being pulled up into the sky."

"I know. All recently deceased are supposed to go up to Heaven first. But I think it would be ok if I took you on a detour for a little while."

I kept my hand on hers and motioned for her to move away from her ascension path and brought her closer to the host of angels who were doing the final descension.

"Come with me," I said, floating toward the descending angels.

"Well Jake Peterson, I never knew you to be someone who breaks the rules."

"I'm not breaking them...Just bending them a little," I said with a laugh.

She laughed, as we hovered right behind the enormous circle of descending angels. I was torn. I wanted to be in the descension *and* be with Katie. Although I was in heaven, being with Katie made it even more heavenly.

While we talked, the legions of angles continued their descension toward earth. Angels had filled in my spot and the circle kept going. There were a few other angels that got out of formation for a bit, but not many.

Katie felt the natural pull of her spirit toward heaven, and I felt a pull to get back into the angelic procession. She could tell.

"You need to go back, don't you?" Katie asked.

"Yes, I do."

"Will I see you again?"

"Yes. Definitely."

"I love you, Jake Peterson!"

"I love you too."

We hovered there together for a minute, spirit hands touching warmly, and nearly oblivious to the sensational activities happening around us. For just a moment, it was only me and her, the stars, and an overwhelming feeling of love.

I didn't want to get back into the descension, but I knew I had to. I floated away slowly, looking at her the whole time as she floated upward, looking down at me.

When I floated back into the processional of angels, I took a new place in the circle, all the while watching Katie's ascension until she floated out of site. I knew I would get to see her again and that made me happy.

As I joined the legion, we glowed with eagerness as we got closer to earth. At the direction of the legion director, we increased our floating radius and sang louder as we moved closer. I saw the destruction that had been taking place for weeks. Piles of rubble where buildings use to be. Rivers and lakes that were dried up. Homes and land that had burned completely. It was devastating. But in a way, it was a type of cleansing of the earth to prepare for the Second Coming.

We got close enough to see people. There were some laying on the ground, and some standing. They looked tired—like they had been through a war with ripped up clothes and many injuries. All of them were looking up at us as we floated closer to them. They were amazed at the sight of billions of angels, glowing, and floating toward them as we sang loudly.

The night sky had turned into day. It gradually became as bright as the sun at noon.

Then, a pillar of light appeared in the center of the circle, shining down even brighter. Brighter than I'd ever imagined. The light fell on all of us—the spirits, the people on earth, the trees, mountains, rivers, and buildings. Everything was touched by the warm light, and it seemed to grow even brighter.

And then...

THE BEGINNING